Treason

Treason

A Catholic Novel
of Elizabethan England

by Dena Hunt

SOPHIA INSTITUTE PRESS
Manchester, New Hampshire

Sophia Institute Press
Box 5284, Manchester, NH 03108
1-800-888-9344

www.SophiaInstitute.com

Sophia Institute Press® is a registered trademark of Sophia Institute

Library of Congress Cataloging-in-Publication Data
Hunt, Dena.
  Treason : A Catholic novel of Elizabethan England / Dena Hunt.
    pages cm
  ISBN 978-1-933184-92-0 (pbk. : alk. paper) 1. Catholics—
England—History—16th century—Fiction. 2. Historical fiction.
I. Title.
  PS3608.U5728T74 2013
  813'.6—dc23
                                                        2013003187

First printing

To Blessed Nicholas Postgate,
a Catholic priest
who faithfully served his "parish"
in the wilds of the Yorkshire moors,
always traveling by foot,
until he was arrested, hanged,
drawn, and quartered at York,
at the age of eighty.

INTRODUCTION

by Joseph Pearce

Good literature takes us out of ourselves and into other worlds. It liberates us from the little provincial cosmos that we have made for ourselves in the limiting confines of our own heads. It takes us on a voyage of discovery of the infinitely wider cosmos that is found beyond ourselves. It shows us a breathtaking and soul-shaking reality that challenges our insular pride and prejudice. It introduces us to the Other, to the Real.

In the realm of so-called fantasy literature ("fantasy" being a poor label for such a great thing), we pass beyond the wardrobe of the self-enclosed mind into the wideness and wonders of an expanding imagination. Yet the wardrobe contains not merely a door of enlarged perception through which we pass but a mirror in which we can see ourselves more clearly. It is in this sense that Tolkien insisted that one of the great values of fairy stories was their ability to hold up a mirror to man. These stories show us ourselves.

What is true of good literature is also true of history. The past is a different country, the visiting of which enables us to see all the more clearly the present day, which is our own small and short-lived country. The past makes sense of the present. It frees us from the fetters of fashion and liberates us from the little prejudiced and provincial cosmos that the zeitgeist presents to us. It shows us the breathtaking and soul-shaking lessons to be learned from the collective experience of humanity over millennia of trial and error. It allows us to learn the lessons without making the mistakes. It is in this sense that the sage reminds us that those who do not learn the lessons of history are doomed to repeat them in the present and are destined to live with their disastrous consequences in the future. The past is a perilous realm in the sense that we ignore it at our peril.

The novel you are about to read brings together good literature and good history, the two becoming one flesh in a nuptial embrace, the fruit of which is a journey to another place that is frighteningly close to home. It shows us ourselves in the lives of our ancestors and reminds us that our forebears are as close to us in their humanity as they are distant from us in time. They are our neighbors whom we are called to love. This novel takes us to a country, Elizabethan England, in which the forces of secularism have outlawed the Catholic Church. It leads us through a political landscape in which the rights of the secular state, as defined by the state itself, trample underfoot the rights of people to follow their conscience and practice their religion. It introduces us to a legal system in which Catholic priests are declared to be traitors to their country and enemies of the people. It shows us a culture of Machiavellian *realpolitik* in which the practice of religion is declared to be a political act and in which the state has established its own church as the only religion to be tolerated.

At its best, Miss Hunt's modest novel resonates with the epic power of *Kristen Lavransdatter* in its unflinching depiction of sanctity in the midst of human folly. Admirers of the great priest-novelist Robert Hugh Benson will find parallels with *Come Rack! Come Rope!* Less obviously but perhaps more palpably, parallels might also be drawn with Benson's apocalyptic and dystopian tour de force, *Lord of the World*. The latter parallel is rooted in the unsettling paradox that history seems to be repeating itself and is now uncannily foreshadowing the future. As such, *Treason* has a Janus-like quality; it looks forward even as it is looking back. It sees the past as a portent of the future, a warning to be heeded. It sees the past as a prophet. Though *Treason* is formally a work of historical fiction, depicting a past that has passed away, it is also, trans-formally, a work of cautionary potency as frightening as Huxley's *Brave New World*, Orwell's *1984*, or the aforementioned *Lord of the World.* It is a work about the past that should be read with one eye on the present and the other on the future. As a manifestation of unchanging truth, the reality that it depicts was and is and is to come.

PREFACE

In the summer of 2006, I had the good fortune to join a Catholic pilgrimage in England for a few days. The pilgrims were led by Father Joseph Fessio, S.J., and Joseph Pearce, renowned biographer and editor of *St. Austin Review*. It was during those few days that I became fully aware of the revisionist history that has been the foundation of my American Protestant heritage.

Among the sites we visited was an ancient tiny church in a sheep pasture outside Keswick in the Lake District—the Church of St. Bega, dating from around A.D. 950. Like all churches in England in the sixteenth century, St. Bega's had its "Reformation" experience: its altar was desecrated, its Bible and prayer books were removed; it was stripped of its small, primitive crucifix, found buried in the sheep pasture only recently; and the murals on its walls, painted by some unknown loving hands, were whitewashed. And like all the other English churches, little St. Bega's became the property of the state.

Father Fessio asked permission to celebrate Holy Mass there, and as each of the small number of pilgrims went forward to receive Holy Communion, I thought about the fact that this was the first time the Blessed Sacrament had been under that roof in nearly five hundred years. Looking back now, I realize that the seed of this story was planted then. I had taught British literature for thirty years, and I was familiar with the rough outline of England's historical attempt, sustained over centuries, to eradicate the Catholic Church. But history tells us only major events and the major persons involved in those events. The little Church of St. Bega made me wonder about the many thousands of unknown persons who were profoundly affected not just by those major events, but by the slow progress of sustained persecution over time. What was it like to live each day in the hope for an end to the "patriotic" religious hatred that forced every citizen to choose between loyalty to country and fidelity to faith? Generations passed on to new generations a hope that was never fulfilled, so that hatred of the Church and all those who remained faithful to her became permanently and inextricably woven into the fabric of England's national character.

As an heir to the Protestant English heritage, I knew well the pervasive legacy of that hatred in American history and culture, but it taxes the imagination to comprehend what life must have been for faithful English Catholics. Interior conflict can be endured for a short time until a resolution is reached, but it can hardly be endured indefinitely, for centuries. Yet it was endured, and the Church survived in England because of it.

The Catholic Church distinguishes two types of martyrdom, represented by two colors: red and white. Red martyrs give their lives for the sake of their faith; white martyrs must bear the Cross each day of their lives. In the face of sustained persecution, fatigue alone would be just cause to surrender, as most of the English did, resolving that interior conflict in the only way they could. But the many thousands of unknown white martyrs of England did not. We know the names of some of the red martyrs, but we know very little of the countless unknown white martyrs of England, those whose faith endured. About them, "official" history makes no mention. This story narrates seven days in the lives of a few of those unknown persons.

All nonhistorical characters and places are fictional; all historical information in the story is accurate to the best of my knowledge. I am very grateful to Professor Jane Kinney of Valdosta State University, for her suggestions of source material; to Elizabeth Paoletti, for her patient reading; to my dear friend Rena Brescia, for her gentle but firm criticism; and to Joseph Pearce, for his near-heroic encouragement.

Dena Hunt

Treason

PROLOGUE

Ordinary, unimportant events can have far-reaching consequences in both space and time. Little decisions, so often made in haste for the sensible purposes of the moment, can affect the lives and fortunes of those in very distant places, and even far into the future. But, with the possible exception of Sheriff Marley, the people of Blexton did not think about such things.

The village lay about half a day's journey east of Exeter in Devonshire. It was a small community of a few hundred souls, made somewhat remote by few roads and a surrounding wood that protected it from the winds that swept the moorland on two sides of it.

Because of that protection and because it was nestled in the middle of a low-lying area below the level of the cliffs that rose above the sea to the south, the soil was free of salt and chalk and was much more fertile than that of the surrounding countryside. In the rest of eastern Devonshire, there was little more to sustain rural folk than sheepherding, but the people of Blexton were farmers in addition to keeping large and fat flocks of sheep — and farmers more prosperous than most. It was rare indeed that any property was available to let. As a result of that happy circumstance, the community kept itself rather insulated as well as isolated. It was a desirable place to live in Devonshire. Most of its inhabitants had lived and prospered there for generations and knew one another well.

The village itself was quite small—a mill, an alehouse, a smith, a wheelwright, an inn, a few shops, and a tannery that was situated on its southwestern edge, thoughtfully downwind of the few dwellings, some of which were occupied by farmers prosperous enough to have residences separate from their farmland that lay some distance outside the village. There was a church, of course—St. Anselm's—and a rectory where the priest, Reverend Andrew Wilson, and his wife resided, not far from the large new manor house of Sir Arnold Somers. Sir Arnold's old house, Somerfield, was leased to a young sea captain, Edward Wingate, and his wife, Caroline. Though Edward was in the Royal Navy, he was not especially fond of the sea and still less fond of the port city of Plymouth. He chose to maintain that distance from Plymouth, with its bustle and constant political intrigue, reckoning that the city and its port were easily reachable by sea from Exeter anyway.

In spring, the area was subject to fairly heavy rainfall, sometimes accompanied by wind from the south. On a night in the late spring of 1581, there was such a rainstorm. Few people of Blexton would know the full consequences of that night's bad weather over the next seven days, not even those who were most directly involved—such as Simon Leacham, whose farm was about six miles east of the village. For Simon, the weather was a matter of deep concern. Simon owned a bull—the only one in the area. To the best of his knowledge, he was the only farmer in all of eastern Devonshire to own a bull, but since he had never traveled farther than Exeter, he wasn't sure about that. It was in Exeter, where his sister lived, that he had spent half his life's savings to buy that bull.

That morning—it was the twentieth of May—Simon had informed his workman John Taversley that he would attend his sister's birthday celebration in Exeter. Worried about his nervous bull, he told Taversley to keep a light burning during the night when he slept in the barn with the bull and the other livestock. Later in the day, however, as the sky darkened, Simon changed his mind about going to Exeter, not trusting his workman to know how to handle a nervous bull. But Simon neglected to tell Taversley about his change of plan.

The structure of the farmhouse was common to that area: livestock and family shared the same roof with only a cross-passage to separate them. Unable to sleep, Simon lit a candle and placed it by the door. Though it was very cold, he went across the passage in his bare feet and opened the door to the barn a crack, pleased to see that Taversley had followed his orders to leave a light burning for the bull. But there he froze in shock. He saw in the dim light of the lantern several people—Taversley, two young men whose faces he could not see from behind, a strange young woman, and a youth—all kneeling in a circle, in the open space across from the double-barred pen where the bull watched in apparent peace. Witches, he knew, formed circles, but they did not kneel—not as far as he knew, anyway. Each of them was holding something in his hands, and all were murmuring some kind of incantation together in low voices, something in a foreign language. He could not understand the words, but he certainly knew they were not English words. Then he understood who they were—not witches, but something almost as bad. They were traitors—and his workman Taversley was the worst among them for his deception of Simon.

He crouched there, peering through the crack in the door, enraged by the treachery of his plowman. What should he do? If he entered the barn yelling—especially with crossbow in hand—they'd escape through the barn door, and the bull might even flee with them if they frightened him enough. True, he kept his matchlock primed and ready by the house door, and the candle was already lit, but he'd get only one of them that way—and he'd make sure it was John Taversley. But then he remembered something else he kept hidden in the chest at the foot of the bed, something he had never told even his wife about, and it was something that didn't have to be primed. By heaven, he wouldn't get them all, but he'd get as many of the traitors as he could — for surely, there was no law against killing spies and traitors. Simon, a very simple man, believed that the spirit of law guided its letter. This unexamined conviction would bring him to grief, but at the moment of decision, his simple loyalty to crown and country made him believe that murder was just. Indeed, it would be no surprise to him if he even got a reward for it.

He stole back across the passage to his bedchamber, and holding the candle in one hand, he threw up the lid of the chest at the foot of the bed with the other. His wife, Lettie, sat up in bed and moved the covers aside.

"Simon! What in heaven's name?"

Simon rummaged through the chest to its bottom and withdrew the treasured weapon. "Hush, woman, and stay abed!"

"But what is that? Simon! What's amiss?"

"Papist spies, Lettie. Enemies!"

1

The twenty-first of May, in 1581

Dawn was arriving in Devonshire. Slow, cold, and gray, like a single drop of water making pale streaks on black paper. It held no promise, not even hope. Neither did the landscape it revealed—barren rocks brooded over by high barren cliffs, swept by cold winds; light was not made welcome there.

A young man trudged along the narrow strand. All the hostile emptiness of that dawn spoke to him: *Go back to the sea; do not come here.* Yet it was like most mornings in his distant memory. It wasn't strange. Why had he not foreseen that it would be like this? In all his memories, plans, and prayers, he had missed this detail—this cold, uniquely English inhospitality to morning. He pulled his cloak closer about him. He must find the path soon. The tide would wash away his footprints from the sand, but he worried that it might not be soon enough, now that dawn was arriving. Not a promising beginning.

Then he thought: no, this will not do. Already I am fearful, and I have only just arrived. He tasted the fear on his tongue, like the cold salt air he breathed. He hated it. Each crash of the swiftly encroaching waves at his back questioned him, accused him: What had really driven him to make this journey—certain to end sooner or later in his death? Was it really his faith? "Perfect faith casts out fear," he knew well. Was what he called faith really only a fear of cowardice, born of vanity and pride? What was it that had really driven him? So many years of preparation,

so many hours in agonized prayer, and he was no nearer the answer to that question than he was at the beginning.

But he could not afford such introspection now—he must
find the path. Daylight and danger were fast approaching.

He looked back toward the sea and saw with relief the empty
horizon. No small feat, considering that only two oarsmen had
had to row against the tide. He felt glad that he had remembered to bless them silently, and he smiled as he recalled that in
the moonless starlight their narrowed eyes and sea-weathered
faces had softened as they saw him make the Sign of the Cross
toward them. One of them had whispered, "*Adieu, Père.* Now
hurry!"

His boots were wet; his feet were numbed by the cold. He
stumbled and fell forward on his hands, and then he saw, just beyond a great sea-beaten boulder ahead, the narrow rocky path. A
few steps more, and he had begun the climb, crouching, glancing
ever upward lest an early fisherman spot the gray cloak moving
among the gray rocks. He looked behind him: the swift tide was
already erasing his footprints. He lowered his head in shame.
How weak and foolish of him to be so fearful. He breathed a
prayer for forgiveness.

Rounding a curve in the path among the rocks, he saw a
bright blue spot ahead, near the top of the cliff. He wondered
at it, so out of place in the endless grayness of land, sea, and
sky. He kept his eyes on it, as though it were a goal, the end of
a dangerous and difficult climb. What was it? When at last he
reached it, he saw that it was a brave little cornflower, strayed
from the fields above. Drenched and drooping, it glanced up at
him sideways from beneath a stone. He smiled. "*Deo gratias.*"
And a second unforeseen thing happened to him then: his eyes
filled with sudden tears and he felt his heart surge within him,
overwhelmed by forgotten love for his homeland, as powerful as
the surging sea behind him. He had not expected that.

* * *

Several miles north of the sea, and just three miles outside the village of Blexton, the small estate of Somerfield drowsed in pre-morning silence, the servants still asleep in their beds. A cold, windy rain had arrived during the night, and Alice, a housemaid, awoke to the sound of a shutter rattling at the end of the kitchen hallway. For a while, she waited irritably for the cook to rise and see to it—her room was closer to the shutter—but finally, in her shift and bare feet, she walked quickly down the hallway, fastened the loose latch, and walked even more quickly back to her warm bed. Not eager to rise and stoke the kitchen fires, she reasoned that Captain and Mrs. Wingate would not rise early on such a morning. The house faced east, and their upstairs bedchambers were at the rear above the gardens. There was no light at all at Somerfield yet, and rooms at the rear of the house would remain in darkness for at least two hours, maybe longer in such bad weather.

But Caroline Wingate was sitting upright in her bed.

"Edward, is it so important to you?" Her voice held just the slightest quaver, but it was enough to make him turn around and look at her. He had been on his way back to his own chamber, but now he stood there in his nightshirt, arrested by that quaver in her voice.

In the dim light of the candle, her head was bowed in shadow. She looked as though she were holding her breath awaiting his answer—which he found he could not give. Her nut-brown curls clung to her white cheek, held there by the dampness of his own sweat. How is it possible, he wondered, for the mere curve of a woman's cheek to break a man's heart?

She raised her tear-filled eyes, an amazing blue, to his, plead-ing. "I do love you," she said in a whisper that was almost a cry.

One hand held the coverlet over her breasts, a reflexive mod-esty that almost made him smile. Her other hand lay resting on top of the coverlet, its palm upward, small, open, and naked; a little round hill, pink and smooth, was just below her thumb. He picked it up and kissed it tenderly, then moved the damp curls from her forehead with his finger. "Do not fret so, my darling. Shall I leave the candle for you?"

"It is a defect in myself." Her chin quivered. "I am sorry. Is it important to you? Edward, I do love you." When he didn't answer, she clasped his hand and held it to her lips. "No, take the candle with you. I will try to sleep now."

He kissed her brow and left her, closing the door softly behind him. Caroline reached down to the floor in the darkness to retrieve her shift with the intention of slipping it over her head, but then she held it to her face and surrendered briefly to silent sobs.

She became aware suddenly that she wanted to be clean. She thought wryly that it was good to desire something, even if it was only a wash. Still weeping, she rose and crossed the room to the washstand. The cold air chilled her moist bare skin. A bit of water was left in the pitcher. She took a cloth from the cupboard, dipped it into the pitcher and bathed her face and then her body, whispering, in a reflex as natural as breathing, "*Credo in unum Deum, Patrem omnipotentem …*" The tears ceased, and what passed for peace in Caroline's soul returned to her.

Across the hall, Captain Edward Wingate pulled the clean sheet and coverlet over himself and snuffed the candle. His passion for his wife surprised him continually; sometimes it even frightened him, as though he were falling into a dark abyss, losing all sight of anything familiar, even himself. Since the first hour of their meeting three years ago, some thought of her, some image, sound, or scent of Caroline had pervaded his consciousness, flooding him with a desire he could not comprehend—unlike any desire he had ever known for a woman. Perhaps a sigh, a slight movement of her shoulder, a fleeting scent—like roses washed in sunlight. Even the sound of her name on his lips. But it was the desire, ever present, that tormented him with sweet pain. He often thought of her as the center of his life, yet he knew vaguely, not understanding what he knew, that it was not Caroline herself, but his own desire that gave his daily life with her an irresistible intensity.

She loved him, yes, but it was the same love she seemed to have for nearly everyone she knew. Not even a small part of her heart was reserved for him alone. Nor did she seem to possess anywhere within her the capacity to feel that love that a woman should feel for a man, and so it never occurred to him to worry whether Caroline might be guilty of infidelity—just as it never occurred to him to examine his own obsessive desire, but only to wonder at her apparent lack of it. Where desire should have been, she loved with deep care, sometimes even sacrifice.

Edward had decided that Caroline's love was the love of a mother, and that her unhappiness was due to the lack of children. If she had a child on whom she could shower her affection, she might find another kind of affection within her—the kind that would be for him alone—as it should be. He frowned. Despite his ardor, Caroline had not conceived. Why?

He knew that the fault lay not with him; he knew of at least two bastards he had left behind him in Coventry before his marriage. But, he thought, they were both conceived by bawdy, rollicking women, full of obvious pleasure. Was it possible that a woman's pleasure was necessary for conception? As naïve as the question seemed, he reflected on the fact that there had never been a need to consider it before.

He decided to ask Beryl. Whores always knew these things. The only difficulty would be in avoiding the cost he might have to pay the lusty woman for that information—a cost not reckoned in money. The thought repelled him, but he'd get around it somehow.

And so it was shortly after midday that Edward sat at table at The Three Lions, waiting. He chafed a bit, being kept waiting, but Maude had whispered to him with a wink and a grin that she would get word to Beryl: "For I know, sir, if she but knew *you* was here, she'd hurry herself up."

He spoke rather absently to the barmaid, "Who is that by the door, Maude?" A young stranger wearing a gray cloak sat in earnest conversation with a farmer Edward recognized as Josiah Braithlow, one of the few known papists in Devonshire. Their voices were too low to hear.

"Him? I don't know, sir. Not rightly, anyways." She placed his ale, in its silver tankard engraved with his crest, on the table at his elbow. "All I know is what Potty says."

"And what does Potty say?"

"He says the man's name is Stephen — Stephen Long, I think he said, or something like that. The Stephen part I'm sure of, but not the other part. He says he's Sir Arnold's new wine steward. But you can never take what Potty says for true, sir, for he's always saying more than he knows, Potty is."

Edward smiled and stretched his stockinged feet closer to the hearth, where his boots stood primly to the side to be kept warm. He glanced at the stranger Stephen Something and thought him a rather pensive fellow. He wondered idly what business Sir Arnold's wine steward should have with Farmer Braithlow — and whether he should employ a wine steward himself. A blustery wet wind entered then with Robert Marley, Sheriff of Devon. He waved a hullo to Edward, who answered with a nod and a smile. Edward did not want companionship just then; he wanted to see Beryl, who was, at this moment, busy upstairs. He hoped his smile toward Robert had been at once both warm and cool. He didn't want Robert to join him, but he didn't want to offend him either. Apparently, the smile had not been quite cool enough. Robert drew up a stool, and Edward noticed that his boots and the bottom of his long dark cloak were covered with mud.

Maude bustled to the table, carrying a mug of ale. "God's Blood, sir! You'll be wanting them boots cleaned, I fancy." Robert nodded and Maude knelt on the floor to struggle with the boots.

"Robert," said Edward, frowning at the mud, "you've surely not been hunting in this weather?"

"God, no!" said Robert, pulling at the fingers of his heavy leather gloves and revealing surprisingly small hands on such a large man. "Nasty bit of business. About six miles east. Some damned fool farmer." Edward raised his eyebrows, and Robert repeated, "Damned fool. Simon Leacham, it was. He'd told his plowman this week past that he would be in Exeter at his sister's birthday last night. But he changed his mind and stayed at home instead. Said he was worried about some nervous bull of his in this foul weather and went to his barn to see to the creature, and there he discovered a nest of papists having some kind of meeting, the plowman among them."

"He sent for you then? Why not the constable?"

"No! In a fit of rage, or so he says, he tried to kill the lot of them. Called them traitors and said he ran back into his house and got a pistol. He got three. Two escaped. What I want to know is how he did that. There's only one way, but where did an old fool like that get a wheel-lock? Only then did it occur to him to send for the constable. It was no case of mere poaching, so he sent for me." He struck the table with his gloves and laid a fisted hand on top of them.

"So, the farmer's in jail now?"

"Oh, aye. But there's the mess. The man's an idiot. What's to be done with him, I'm sure I don't know. He may have saved bother to the Crown—but it doesn't end there. No one knows who the woman was that he killed. Worse, she appears to be gentry. The other, her servant perhaps, and then there's the plow-man, John Taversley. And God knows who it was that got away. The plowman's dead, of course, so he can't help us." He took the tankard Maude handed him, drank it down in what appeared to be one swallow, then lifted it to signal for another. "Damned fool. The whole thing is too much mystery for me. I've decided myself on it. I'll send a report to the Queen's Commission and forget the matter until somebody tells me what to do with the idiot farmer. And I'll just forget about the two escapees."

"But what will you do about the lady?"

"I don't know. I suppose we'll know who she was when somebody reports her missing."

"Then how will you explain that, if you end up letting Leacham go?"

"I haven't come to that part yet. God knows. For I'm sure I don't."

Nasty business indeed. But then Edward saw Beryl descend-ing the stairs, and he nodded to her. He had other business to attend just now and wasn't interested in Robert's problem. Catching his nod, Beryl paused on the stairs, made a coy little curtsy, and turned with a smug smile to go back to her room. Edward rose to follow in his stocking feet, leaving behind boots, ale, and Robert, who seemed very surprised by Edward's ascent up the stairs with Beryl.

The room was tiny, just large enough for a sagging bed, a small cupboard, a rough wooden table, and a stool. There was one narrow window, which, unfortunately on this rainy day, was shut. The room stank of sex. He stopped her when she started to undress. "No, Beryl. I was thinking by the fire just now that you should have a rest sometimes. You stay busy so much, we seldom see you below stairs. What if we just chat a bit?"

Beryl fought back a sigh. She was disappointed. The thought of entertaining the handsome Captain Wingate had excited her.

She had even had a little wash and applied some scent. She thought perhaps he might need a bit of encouragement on his first private visit with her.

"Oh, now, Captain. How kind you are." She took him by the shoulders and guided him to the stool. "Just sit yourself down here now. Beryl'll sit in your lap, yes — just like this — and now you just chat as long as you like."

She ran her fingers through his dark blond hair, which fell back in heavy waves from his clean-shaven face, lightly browned by sun and sea. He put his right arm around her waist and rested his hand on her thigh, but he leaned his left arm on the table. away from the threatening bosom. and made an effort at a thin chuckle. "You do enjoy your bed, don't you, old girl?"

"Oh, aye, Captain. No complaints from me. And Maude is good to me, she is. Feeds me good and never takes more than her share of my earnings." *What did the blighter want?*

"Ah, then, you must have a right brood of little bastards somewhere?"

She laughed. "What do you mean, sir? I've got me own ways of handling that problem. And anyways, that would be telling now, wouldn't it?" She twirled his hair in her fingertips and toyed with his ear. *What was in his mind? Had he got some lady pregnant who's not his wife? And the wench don't know what to do?*

"Well, I have heard it said that women who enjoy their men get children by them. Is that so?"

"Well, now, as I said, sir, that would be telling." She dropped her hand from his neck and ear; suspicion crept in at the edges of her thought: *No, that's not his problem — more like somebody's not pregnant — and he thinks* ... "Are you wanting to know, then, Captain, what makes a woman enjoy her man? I can tell you this much, sir, *any* woman would enjoy *you* — any *real* woman, anyways." But as she looked on her rumpled bed with the disappointed certainty that there would be no fun there today with

Captain Wingate, she could hardly suppress the laughter that threatened to erupt.

For his part, Edward thought she did not understand his question, distracted as she was by a desire to "teach" him how to please. He was not interested in how to please, but in whether conception required it. It was clear that neither his desire nor Beryl's would be fulfilled by this encounter.

"Oh, I just remembered, old girl. Can't stay, after all. I do think there's a leg of mutton waiting for me below stairs." He slapped her thigh and pushed her up with his knees. She didn't want to move, so he stood, almost dropping her off his lap. "But here's for your time." He tossed a few pence from a leather purse on the table.

"Oh, now, Captain. Have you got to be going so soon?"

Another false chuckle. "I've another sort of hunger." And he was gone from the room, leaving Beryl standing there, with the conflicting impulses of disappointment and amusement—for Beryl had understood what he wanted to know. The latter impulse won, and she laughed aloud as she shoved her bosom back into her bodice.

Below stairs, Robert was deep into a leg of mutton himself. He glanced up at Edward, descending the stairs far too soon for any real business with Beryl to have been accomplished, and he wondered what Edward had wanted with her. He knew Edward's devotion to Caroline. But Edward only nodded farewell to him and signaled to Maude to bring his boots and cloak. He sat down on the bench by the door and pulled on his boots, stood, and fastened his cloak, glancing, as he passed, at the young stranger Stephen Something, still in conversation with Farmer Braithlow.

Outside in the cold wet wind, he stamped his boots in impatience and frustration over the failure of his mission as he waited for Potty to bring him the reins of his horse. Then he mounted, spurred his horse harder than necessary, and headed for home.

Upstairs, Beryl went without pausing to the small chest she kept under her bed, and still giggling to herself about Captain Wingate's "problem," she withdrew a small piece of dirty paper, an inkpot, and quill and sat down at the little table. She was hungry for her own dinner, but it must wait.

* * *

"The post came while you was out, sir." The housemaid Alice held out a tray of polished pewter to Edward. He retrieved two letters from it and handed one of them to Caroline, who sat on the other side of the table, spread for his late dinner. "Your aunt has written again, my dear."

He noted the Crown seal on his own letter and opened it at once. He read quickly and frowned: It seemed that he would be drawn into Robert's "nasty bit of business." Word had evidently reached the Commission in London of a group of papists in Devon, and Edward was instructed to look into the matter. He knew how the Commission would have heard about such a group—if indeed there was one. Lord Walsingham's network of spies reached far beyond England's own borders into all of Europe and even into the New World. But his frown deepened as he tried to think of some reason for his own involvement—the business had nothing to do with him. What was he expected to do about it? It wasn't even an affair for Robert, really—at least, not yet—but for the bishop. But perhaps the bishop had already been informed. In any case, there was no reason Edward should be involved.

He stood and paced before the hearth, where a cheerful fire might have comforted him in the small but pleasant dining hall of Somerfield. Still holding the letter before him at the level of his eyes, he stared above it at the tapestry on the wall opposite the fire, depicting a wild-boar hunt, and lost himself in the puzzle, unaware of Caroline's observation. She was seated with her hand resting on the table, on top of her own letter, which remained unopened.

Past his initial confusion about his involvement, he wondered how he might handle the situation now that Whitehall was involved. Questions raced through his thoughts. The Commission could not know about the killings at the Leacham farm; that had happened only last night. Perhaps all that would be needed now was a simple written report of what had already transpired, and that report might put an end to their inquiry. In any case, that was Robert's job, not his.

Why had he been informed at all? Was he expected to pursue the two escapees? That would mean the awkward business of searching—fruitlessly, no doubt—the countryside, the villagers' houses. Even if the escapees were found, could the slow-witted farmer now in jail identify them? And there would also be the problem of identifying the dead, a necessary detail now. Then it occurred to him to wonder what disposition Robert would make of the bodies. He regretted now his preoccupation during Robert's exposition of the incident. He must talk with him right away.

He refolded the letter and glanced out the window. It was almost dusk, and there was still a cold, blowing rain. Nevertheless, he would have to send for Robert to come at once. He silently repeated Robert's curse of the farmer: *damned fool.* What would Robert do about the bodies? Perhaps with a bit of luck, and some consultation with the jailed farmer, the two escapees could be forgotten. That would be in everyone's best interest, even the farmer's.

Edward was not eager to pursue two fleeing Catholics, not particularly because he had any sympathy for the fugitives— though he did—but simply because he felt that such a pursuit had nothing to do with him as a commissioned officer in the queen's navy.

Edward did not like to be involved in political matters at all. As for religion, he was indifferent. Privately, he thought the subject was an entirely political matter to the queen, having nothing to do with religion itself, which he believed was superfluous to her outside its obvious usefulness in arousing national pride—especially, perhaps, in view of the Catholic Scottish queen's more legitimate claim to the throne. Elizabeth had made herself, the country, and the "Church of England" into a single object for the devotion and loyalty of the English people. Unfortunately for English Catholics, that required a view of them as enemies of the state, as "papists" and traitors.

He attended the queen's church every Sunday; the law required his attendance, and it was the proper thing for a man of his standing to do. But on the whole, he thought the laws against Catholics very foolish in the long view—if the queen had done what was better for England than for herself. What was better for England, it seemed obvious to him, would be tolerance for Catholics, to be on the pope's good side, rather than making him an unnecessary enemy, as the queen had done. England had enough enemies in France—and always in Scotland—and now Spain as well, due to her harassment. He knew, however, that his opinions on that subject were best kept to himself.

He sighed, annoyed by the whole affair, and very confused about his own involvement. He resolved to speak to Robert immediately.

"Alice," he spoke to the servant, still standing in the doorway, sensing further orders. "Tell Joseph to ride to Sheriff Marley—he's at The Three Lions—and tell him that I must see him this very evening."

She dipped a curtsy. "Yes, sir."

Across the table, Caroline still held the unopened letter from her Aunt Margaret. She had noted her husband's deep frown, his agitation, and then the command to summon Sheriff Marley. "Edward," she asked tentatively, "is something wrong?"

He made an effort to turn from his troubling thoughts and give her a small smile. "Nothing that should concern you, my dear. Now. What news does your aunt have to relate from Somerset?"

"Ah," she replied, remembering the letter she held. She opened it and was surprised by her aunt's first sentence: "Dearest Caroline, We are unblessed by your long absence." The awkward term *unblessed* first confused, then worried her. She read the brief letter quickly. What did Aunt Margaret mean? The rest of the letter merely asked her to visit and gave news of her cousin Eleanor's journey. She decided to speak to Edward about the possibility of visiting her aunt, but not now, when he was clearly concerned about another matter—better to wait until this concern passed and his mood might be more generous. She knew well Edward's preference that she not visit her family often.

"Nothing important. She speaks of Eleanor's trip. I won't bother you with it now."

Edward's scowl deepened. His day had been frustrating, much like the miserable weather outside. He did not completely approve of his wife's having so much correspondence with members of her family. It was one of their peculiarities to educate their daughters in much reading and writing. He had often thought that it was perhaps the custom of all such families engaged in commerce. Their rising wealth gave them the means to hire tutors, and so they overeducated their daughters, doubtless ignorant of the customs of landed families like his own, to whose status—he took for granted—the merchant class aspired. They would never achieve it, of course; no amount of wealth could substitute for birth. But the subject of birth sent him deeper into gloom. He made an effort to appear interested. "Where has your cousin Eleanor gone this time?" He thought it unseemly that a young woman should travel so often, even if she were escorted.

"Aunt Margaret doesn't say. Edward, since Sheriff Marley will be visiting you this evening, I am inclined to retire early, if that is agreeable to you?" She was very tired, having had little rest the night before, but mostly she wanted to be alone to think about Margaret's meaning of *unblessed* without distraction. It was like her aunt to be sensible of the fact that letters sent to Caroline might be read by her husband. They were never more than greetings and small news of the family, the kind of news Margaret knew Edward would find uninteresting. But to use the awkward phrase "we are unblessed" was not at all like her, and Caroline found herself somewhat concerned.

Edward's attention was elsewhere. "Hm? Oh, certainly, my dear." But his face softened as he looked at her, so lovely in a plain, unadorned gown of pale blue silk, looking up at him with perfect deference in her waiting expression.

She rose, and taking her letter with her, kissed her husband's cheek. "Good night, Edward." She left him staring into the fire, his dinner forgotten.

He was glad for once of Caroline's absence, leaving him free to think about his own letter without distraction. Why had Whitehall not written to the bishop instead? This was not a military matter—at least not for the navy. The entire country had just been levied a second time to raise militia for the purpose of pursuing Catholic priests, believed to be hiding among the papists, and for punishing "recusancy," the refusal of some Catholics to attend the services of the English national church. But there was no need for the navy in this pursuit. What did the Crown intend? Deprived of position or authority, and most of their fortunes, all Catholics with any influence had already been driven underground; that should suffice for the purposes of the state. But now the expensive militia had been established to root them out. Why was there such urgent need to fear a religion already suppressed? Of course, there was the threat of Mary, Queen of Scots, legitimate heir to the throne and Catholic …

Just then, Alice rushed back into the dining hall carrying another letter. "I beg pardon, sir. When I gave your order to Joseph just now, he gave me this for you. He says it came by a courier yesternight after you went to bed, and he had no chance to get it to you till now because you were out."

The letter had the same seal. He snatched it from her hand. "Why was this not brought to me this morning?" He fought an impulse to send for Joseph to chastise him; he didn't want to delay the servant's departure to bring Robert.

"I don't know, sir, I'm sorry, he didn't say more, sir." Alice retreated quickly.

Edward tore at the large red seal on the folded parchment. Then he had to read the document twice to make sure he had not misread it. He sat down slowly in the high-backed chair by the fire. The council had bypassed the aldermen, bypassed, it would seem, all normal procedure. He had been appointed magistrate, and he was to assume authority immediately on receipt of the letter. At first, he felt both surprise and honor; he wondered if his father, who spent a good deal of time at Court, had been instrumental in the appointment. That would be very like him. But then his apprehension returned: Why such haste in the appointment? What did that haste signify?

Whatever the reason, this news explained his involvement. It also altered his intentions in meeting with Robert. With growing relief, he realized there would be no need for his own participation in pursuit of the fugitives. Indeed, the sheriff would hold all that responsibility without him. It occurred to him that Robert would now be under his authority, and the thought made him smile. He and Robert were hunting companions and friends; it amused him to think that Robert might now be answerable to him. But, in truth, in whatever lay ahead, Edward wanted as little real involvement as possible; he would simply cooperate with Robert and pass whatever judgment was necessary. There would be little enough for him to do, except to hold the honor of the position of magistrate.

Upstairs, Caroline prayed fervently before she went to bed, having understood finally that *unblessed* probably meant that Kefington, the village near her aunt's estate in Somerset, must have had another visitation from the High Commission. She prayed that no one in the village was harmed. She knew that if any of her family had been involved, she would have been informed directly.

Apart from her father, who lived far away in Yorkshire, her Aunt Margaret Anders and her two cousins in Somerset were all the family she had, now that her mother was dead. Indeed, Andersgate had been more her home than York since the death of her mother. She prayed that Edward would give his permission for her to make the journey to Andersgate, for now she felt that she must ask him right away, especially since Eleanor was away from home and her Aunt Margaret was likely to be alone and frightened by the visitation. In fact, she could almost feel her aunt's fear for Eleanor's safety in her words. Her other cousin, Margaret's son, John, was often away on business. She prayed for her family's safety. She prayed God's forgiveness for her own safety. She prayed for her husband. And last, as always, she prayed to be delivered from her life. A life of deceit, a life in exile from her own heart.

* * *

At The Three Lions, Sheriff Marley had lit his pipe and leaned back in his chair to enjoy a short while of fireside talk with his men. Good food and good ale, he reflected, can change any bad situation for the better. He had decided to write his report when he went home that evening and, in the meantime, to for-get about the "nasty business" in Leacham's barn. Then he saw Edward's Joseph stamping his muddy shoes in the doorway and shaking the rainwater from his cap. Even before the servant headed in his direction, he knew somehow that his relaxation was over before it started—something was amiss at Somerfield.

Joseph bowed. "Beg pardon, my lord sheriff." He waited to be answered before continuing.

"What's amiss, Joseph?" Robert asked in open irritation.

"Captain Wingate asks, please you, sir, to come to Somer-field as soon as may be."

"Now? This evening?"

"Yes, sir. As soon as may be," Joseph repeated.

Robert didn't answer right away. He was annoyed. "Very well." He sighed. "Tell him I will be there in an hour or so."

"Thank you, sir. I'll tell the captain you'll be coming right away." He bowed and turned back to the door, pushing the wet cap down on his head again.

"Damnation," muttered Robert. If something was wrong, why did Edward not speak with him earlier, when he was there at the inn? The weather was foul. He wanted to finish his pipe, to go home and write the damned report, to have a brandy with his wife, Louise, and settle down next to her plump and pleasant body in bed. But his conscience pricked him—perhaps some-thing was really wrong. Edward Wingate was his friend. He tapped out his pipe on the hearth and raised a finger to signal Maude to bring his boots, told his companions he had business at Somerfield, and prepared to leave.

Mounting his tall bay outside, Robert wondered about Edward's strange brief visit with Beryl, whether it could be connected to whatever was wrong. If so, it would be an odd con-nection indeed. What would a whore have to do with trouble at Somerfield? He had a mind given to puzzlement, well suited for his position. It had often seemed to him that everything is connected, one way or another, sooner or later. He wouldn't be surprised to find a connection between whatever was happening at the Wingate household now and the nasty business at the Leacham farm last night. Stupid farmer.

* * *

Quite late that night, Edward retired to his study to write some notes for his report—his first, he mused pleasantly, as magistrate. As he wrote, he reflected with some contentment on his new authority.

Enjoying several brandies along with the news of his appointment, Edward and Robert had decided together that the bodies left in Farmer Leacham's barn should simply be burnt, though that clever suggestion had been Edward's alone, actually. Leacham's testimony recording the events on his farm would be written tomorrow and sent to the Commission in the magistrate's letter. Robert's report would concur in all respects.

They agreed that, on balance, if the farmer were released from jail, such clemency would certainly persuade him to forget the two escapees. They spoke openly about the injustice of not punishing the farmer for murder, but that injustice would be necessary in order to forestall further injustice. Robert commented that his wife, Louise, would be appalled enough, as it was, that the murders had occurred at all, but even more appalled that the farmer should go unpunished. Edward replied that though Caroline had no interest in such matters, he was sure she would agree, and the two men ruminated sagely on the foolishness of Parliament—there in distant London, making laws to advance their own political gain without a care for the trouble those laws caused for those in the country who must enforce them. And Robert left, quite late and equally contented, aware that all would be well for him under the new magistrate.

* * *

Meanwhile, Potty Deeters stood in the darkness outside the back door of the rectory. He was dripping wet after his hurried trip from The Three Lions, protecting Beryl's little note, folded many times and wrapped in leather under his tunic. He was waiting for Mistress Wilson, wife of the Reverend Mr. Andrew Wilson, to return. He had handed her the note, which she took from him at the doorway with the thumb and forefinger of her left hand. He thought she was taking a very long time to return. Probably she was reading the note and measuring its worth. He himself could not read, and he never knew the value of any note he delivered; he could judge its worth only by what he received for its delivery.

Now the parson's wife returned and dropped *half a crown* into his hand, careful as always not to touch the grimy palm. Then she closed the door in his face, very quietly, without a sound, without a word of thanks or regard.

* * *

Only half an hour's ride from the Leacham farm, where three bodies still lay as they had fallen, next to a fenced-off pen of new spring lambs, was a farmstead that belonged to a man named Josiah Braithlow. There an exhausted young priest slept fitfully, having been put to bed just after supper, with a warm woolen blanket, in the fresh, dry straw in a loft above the livestock. From that same farm, a rider had already set out early that morning, heading toward Bath with the heavy news of what had happened at Simon Leacham's farm to those who had been sent to meet the priest. Now the priest would have to wait until the rider returned with the only good riding horse the Braithlow family had. Until then, his presence would put the family in grave danger.

2

Caroline's aunt Margaret had risen early, unable to sleep. Now she sat by the hearth and squinted over the fine stitches of her embroidery in the dim morning firelight. She had punctured her fingers so many times that she finally laid the needlework down in her lap; the linen already had on it several tiny dots of blood, which would have to be removed before she continued anyway. Sewing had not helped; the red spots on the white cloth only reminded her of the very thing she had taken up the needlework to forget — or, if not forget, at least to remove from the forefront of her mind. How she wished her son, John, were home. He had gone to Manchester on business and would likely not return for a few days more. And her daughter, Eleanor, was away on another of her messenger errands. But after what had happened in the village, she could only be grateful for her absence, even though any thought at all of Eleanor now only formed a hard knot of fear inside her chest — so tight that she could hardly breathe. Eleanor had left five days ago, and Margaret still had not heard from her, not a word to let her know that she was safe.

She was alone. She always felt her widowhood most keenly in the absence of her children, but now she felt the loss of her husband as though it were fresh. Ben had been dead these past ten years, but today, it was as if he had died yesterday. If only John were home, she'd not feel her weakness so pervasively, her fear so sharply.

The day after Eleanor left, the village of Kefington had been subjected to a visitation from the High Commission. Margaret thanked God that her spirited, strong-willed daughter had already left when it happened. There had been no warning—*why had there been no warning?*—and two women in the village had been found with the old Catholic prayer books; one of them was also found in possession of a deadly incriminating priest's chasuble. Accused of harboring a priest and sentenced under the Bill of Attainder, Kate Pettigrew had been hanged without trial, in the public square, amid revilements too horrible to remember—the vicar, the churchwardens, and the soldiers all shouting, calling for the death of all "traitors to crown and country."

The simple people of Kefington, awed by the unexpected presence of the queen's own bishops, at first stood by in dumbstruck silence. Finally, roused by the accusations of "treason," they shouted their own newly found hatred, calling for the death of Kate Pettigrew, an old woman they'd known all their lives, a woman who had given her sons and husband to service for the country and was now left alone, defenseless, accused of treason for being found with a priest's vestment in her house. No further evidence was needed, the bishops declared—clearly, the woman had been hiding a popish priest. The sentence was extraordinary; it was obvious to Margaret that the Commission had determined beforehand that some example must be made. Perhaps the queen had felt that her declared "tolerance" was being abused in Somerset. It was true that there were a good many recusants there, and perhaps the Commission had felt that papists in that county should be suppressed still more. Certainly the local church had been full to bursting last Sunday to hear the anti-Catholic sermon. The lesson had been learned.

Margaret had forced herself to attend the execution so that Mrs. Pettigrew could see her face in the crowd and feel her prayer. The hateful obscenities, shouted against "devilish pop-ery" in general and Kate Pettigrew in particular, had blessedly dissolved from her memory. At the moment of the hanging, Margaret had closed her eyes, so she did not have to recall that gruesome sight; her only memory was of Kate looking into her eyes across the crowd's ugly distorted faces, and seeing there, or so Margaret hoped, sympathy and compassion. It was all she could do.

The irony was that Margaret knew well Kate Pettigrew was not even Catholic. Many years ago, during the reign of young Edward, the first visitation had stripped the church of cruci-fixes, chalices, pictures, and even small statues, to rid them of all vestiges of "popish superstition" and make the church "Eng-lish." There was a great bonfire of religious articles and prayer books. Some of the people had managed to hide a few of the beautiful and beloved things, usually by burying them in the ground, but some had unwisely hidden them in their houses, not knowing then that other visitations would follow. A few years ago, when the Commission last visited their little church, they found no incriminating evidence of "foreign religion," but Kate had likely got hold of a chasuble somehow and kept it only because she thought it beautiful, perhaps wanting to use the lovely fabric.

Finally, Margaret gave up any attempt to embroider, any at-tempt to stop the fear. Still holding the needle in her right hand, she placed her left hand over her eyes, pressing it against her lids to clear the tears. But she must not cry. Her servant Eloise could enter at any moment and find her weeping. In Margaret's overwhelming fear at that moment, she was sure that any wit-ness of her sorrow would immediately find her guilty of being a Catholic — and she would be hanged forthwith. "O Lord," she prayed almost aloud, "where is Father Joseph? Please keep him safe!" He had disappeared just before the visitation. She prayed earnestly that he was safely hidden somewhere. As if in confir-mation of her fears, Eloise entered and asked, "Shall I bank the fire now, madam?"

"Yes, please." She stood and began untying her pinafore apron. "And bring my cloak, Eloise. I think I will visit Mistress Smith."

"Oh, ma'am, that's a lovely thing to do. How she must feel just now! I do hope other folk have visited her, but I have doubt of it—her being Mistress Pettigrew's friend and all—and never mind her having one of them books, too."

"Well, most probably not. Everyone is still in shock."

"Hm. You couldn't tell no shock from what I saw of them yell-ing for poor Mistress Pettigrew's hanging! And just fancy—all for having a bit of cloth in her house! Will you ride, ma'am?"

"No, I'll walk." She suddenly felt that she could not get out of the house fast enough.

"Mind your boots, ma'am. It's still damp out. Will you be back for dinner?"

Margaret took the cloak Eloise held open for her. "Oh, yes. But there's only me, so just some of that soup from yesterday, please, and a bit of bread."

Eloise banked the fire in the hearth after her mistress's de-parture. She thought her such a kind lady to be thinking of poor old Mistress Smith now. Likely nobody else would be thinking of her. Even if they did, they'd be too ashamed to see to her, after what they'd done.

The whole business was sorry. She sighed. What had got it into the queen's head to worry herself about the pope? He lived so far away in another country. Wasn't being queen of England enough for her? Eloise was not a religious person and knew little about it, but she understood a thing or two about women, be-ing one herself. The queen was queen, yes, but she was still a woman—and what a woman wanted was a man in her bed.

That would set her to rights, it would. It would make her forget all this nonsense about being the pope of England.

* * *

Margaret closed the sheepgate behind her. As soon as her foot touched the pasture grass, her head lifted and her eyes rose to the green hills that surrounded her, especially the one to her left, referred to by the people of Kefington as Gaston Hill. It was small, compared with its neighbors. Perhaps only because it was the nearest, or perhaps because her eyes inevitably focused on the wide rill that ran from its summit down below the line of her vision—she didn't know why, but when she raised her eyes, they always went to Gaston Hill first, to the silver ribbon that flowed down its center. The small dark copse on her right, the great hills still shrouded in morning mist, the clean, cool air that filled her whole being, even the cowslips and daisies at her feet—all of it, as always, cleared her mind and eased her heart. It was impossible not to pray: *Thank you, my God. Thank you for my being, for the being of all that is around me.*

And thus it began. Walking and praying had always been synonymous for Margaret, especially at morning, her favorite time of day. So deep was her bond with the land that she had often prayed to die there. *If possible, Lord, at morning. Let this be the last sight I see, the last air I breathe.* She was not native to this part of England. She had been brought there as a young bride of seventeen from York, a child of a family of wool merchants named Nelson, and used to city streets. Why on earth Ben Anders had fallen in love with her she had never understood. His family had occupied Andersgate for nearly three hundred years. She could not imagine what it would be like to have three centuries of this country running through one's veins. Ben Anders could not know when he married her that the country to which he would take his bride would rival himself in her heart. Then one day, on just such a walk as this one, she understood that her love for Ben and for these hills was the same love. Things always became clear on her walks.

She passed the poplar that marked the beginning of the path that would ultimately lead down to the village, and as always, she reached out her right hand to caress its leaves as she passed. It was the doorpost of the wood she entered, a vast cathedral of ancient forest with its choirs of morning birdsong, and as always, her tread became softer, slower, more reverent. And then, as it often happened, her soul grew quiet, unable to speak at all. Words were mere cups trying to contain the heavens. She glanced upward from time to time as she walked, to see the leaves moving against the sky in the morning breeze, like a hymn made visible.

At length the cluster of thatched roofs that was Kefington came into view below, but her mind would not move forward to her planned visit with Mrs. Smith. It moved instead to Caroline. She hoped with all her heart that her niece's husband would allow her to visit now. Caroline's presence in the house was like being here in the woods. It was the universe in order; it was God in his Heaven; it was peace in the world. Whenever Caroline arrived at Andersgate—even when she was still a child—it was as though grace itself had crossed its threshold, and never did her niece's arrival go unmarked by Margaret as a blessing.

She tried to hope Caroline had found happiness in her marriage, but she knew that it could never be so. Her brother William had made a serious mistake—no, it wasn't a mere mistake, but a sin—when he insisted that Caroline marry Edward Wingate. Edward was a good man, but he could never rival the Spouse that would always reign in Caroline's heart. William had lost his beloved wife only a few years before, and Caroline was all he had left; he could not bear the thought of losing her to the abbey in France—where he would never see her again. The error had compounded itself when he chose to marry her to a Protestant, though he believed his decision would ensure her safety. How little he knew his daughter. He could not know the depth, the power, and the strength of the vocation to which she had been called. Margaret sighed. He couldn't know her because he didn't know himself, didn't understand that his "love" for his daughter was her cross. She could not disobey him—it wasn't in her. And now her husband's love was another cross, one that would eventually break her completely unless some kind of miracle could save her.

No. No, not yet. Margaret was not ready for the village, for Mrs. Smith. She turned and retraced her steps until the village could be thought remote, distant, until her duty could be seen as "not yet." She was in an enclosure of tall pines and saw woodland violets at her feet. She felt, as she had before, an almost mystical kinship with them. They were hidden here, as she was herself, in the deepest part of the forest, unseen, undesiring of being seen. She spread her cloak on the ground and lay down, looking upward at the patches of sky among the pine tops. *My God, let me die here now. No, not until Eleanor is safe and John is well married. And then, my Lord, when it's time, bring me here and let me stay.*

She closed her eyes and remembered the night, some five months after her marriage to Ben, when she'd awakened beside him. Seeing the starlight through the open shutter, she felt a desire that seemed to her irresistible. Almost without thinking, she rose and went outside in her shift and sat down on the green pasture, turning her face to the stars, feeling her whole being alive in their presence. Then she felt, without fear or surprise, Ben's hand on her shoulder, and she turned to him with tears in her eyes and said, "My darling husband. I fear—oh, Ben, I fear—that I love this place more than I love you!" He said nothing but held her in his arms as she turned her face again to the starlit heavens.

She smiled now, looking up at that same sky where small white clouds drifted instead of stars, and remembered the day a few years ago when she and John were walking through that pasture; she'd paused at the edge of it and said, "You were conceived here, you know, John." He blushed, surprised and embarrassed by her remark.

It had occurred to her sometime after Ben's death while he was on a business trip to Liverpool that she should wish his body buried here, but she had never wished it so. Why? Perhaps because if there had been a grave here, she'd feel somehow differently, and she was content as it was to feel that wherever she went around Andersgate, under daylight or starlight, he was there — not in a grave, but with her.

Quite suddenly, she heard a loud cawing and opened her eyes to see a large crow flying overhead in the direction of the village. She sat up quickly and refastened her cloak, stood and continued her journey into Kefington, walking briskly.

* * *

"Oh, Mistress Anders! How grand to see you. Please do come in, ma'am." Mrs. Smith made a curtsy at her doorway and stood back to allow Margaret to enter her small house at the edge of the village. She hastily tried to tuck straying gray hairs under her cap and smooth her apron. "Please do come in," she repeated, "please, sit here by the fire." She rushed to move a cat from one of the two chairs in the small room.

"Thank you, Mrs. Smith. Yes, well, I was just doing an errand or two and thought you might be able to spare a few minutes for a little visit."

"Oh, my. Oh, my, well—yes ma'am." She took Margaret's cloak and hung it on a peg by the door. "Please do sit down," she said again and patted the back of the cat's chair. "Nobody is come since—"

Margaret settled in the chair. "How cozy it is here, Mrs. Smith. Oh, I see you're doing the same sort of pattern that I am trying to do." She picked up an embroidery hoop from the table beside her. "I have so much trouble with this stitch just here. I simply cannot seem to make it do. I believe I've removed the thread a dozen times. But you have done it quite nicely."

"Oh, well, ma'am, it's really quite easy. You see, you just have to make a few small knots to make the round." Her thumbnail went across the knots to demonstrate.

"Now, why did I not think of that? I see. That allows the thread to continue around the curve without making an ugly angle. I shall have to remember how you've done it."

Mrs. Smith moved the only other chair to face Margaret with the small, cold hearth to her left side. Margaret could see the strain, the fear almost embedded in the old woman's wrinkled face. From the corner of her eye, she noted the disarray of the room, cupboards standing open, dirty pots and bowls on the hearth, and the stale odor of cabbage soup cooked some days ago. The windows had not been opened to air out the house. She should have come before now.

"Well, what do you know, Mrs. Smith. I have heard that Sir Henry is planning a great feast at Rogationtide this year to be had on the green. Have you heard aught about it? My Eloise tells me that it will surpass anything we've yet seen."

"No, ma'am. I've not been into the village this past week."

"But you are planning to take part in Rogationtide, are you not?"

"Well, I don't know. I have not thought— Oh, ma'am!" She picked up the tail of her apron and held it to her face. "Nobody will see me, Mistress Anders. Nobody is even spoke to me since Kate—" She sobbed into her apron.

Margaret's hand reached across the little table between them and held the old woman's shaking shoulder.

"I didn't know Kate was a papist traitor, Mistress Anders. I never would have been friends with her if I knew that. She gave me that little book, and I kept it because it was the only book I ever owned. But, Mistress Anders, how was I supposed to know it was one of them evil Mass books? I can't read! And truth to tell, I didn't know Kate could neither, but I guess she could if she had one of them books. But she never told me that, and she never told me what that book was. I never would have kept it!"

The old woman's disloyalty to her friend made Margaret's heart sink. "Well, Mrs. Smith, maybe she didn't know what it was either." Of that Margaret was certain, just as she was certain that Kate had no way of understanding what a crime it was to possess a priest's vestment.

"Oh, but she had to know, ma'am. She was a papist!"

It was clear to Margaret that Mrs. Smith, along with the queen's bishops, had condemned and hanged her friend. This apparently lesser tragedy seemed to be a poisonous aftertaste of the greater one, and she supposed she should have expected it. But perhaps in the longer view, this betrayal would turn out to be the far greater tragedy in the end: Mrs. Smith would find it necessary to condemn her friend, not just in order to regain acceptance among the village folk, but to be able to accept the murder of Kate Pettigrew as just and right. It was the law—the law of England. And it was Her Majesty's own holy bishops. The Church had been outlawed; that voice had been silenced. There was no greater moral authority for the common, ordinary people of England. Kate was guilty; her punishment was just. Margaret felt a catch in her throat, a missed beat in her heart, overwhelmed with pity.

"Now, Annie Smith, let me help you get your hair under your cap. Have you a clean apron? You and I will go to market together. I need some more thread, and our cook Maybelle told me to get half a dozen turnips. Have you some clean water handy? Let's bathe that face of yours."

All of this only made Mrs. Smith sob the louder, but presently she settled, wiped her nose on her apron, and rose to comply with Margaret's commands. "Mistress Anders, you are the finest lady, finer, I declare, than Lady Henry herself!"

Margaret rose to help. "Nonsense. Now where's your water bucket? Here it is." She took a cloth from the open cupboard, dipped it in the water and handed it to the old woman. "Bathe your face now while I repair your hair."

When all preparations were made, a clean apron located and donned, the two women slipped out the door. As they approached the market, Margaret chattered about the size of the turnips, just the right color of thread, and whatever else she could think of. There were few people at the market so late in the morning, but those who were there took careful note of the women, of the friendliness of wealthy and well-respected Mistress Anders with the rejected village woman. They knew the two women were not really friends. Margaret's purpose was obvious, and a few had the grace to allow a small shadow of shame to cross their faces.

Margaret knew that Annie Smith's ostracism was over, but as they passed the place where the hastily erected gallows still stood, she saw the woman's body begin to tremble and feared she would collapse again into sobbing. She slipped her arm around her waist and gave just the slightest squeeze. "Oh, Mrs. Smith, do come and help me choose the right shade of green for the leaf on that stitchery I told you of." Mrs. Smith regained her composure, and eventually, during their shopping, she even managed a few nervous smiles.

Back on the forest path on the way home to Andersgate, Margaret stopped and discarded the turnips for the wild creatures to enjoy. She sat down near the place where she had lain earlier and had watched the leaves overhead so joyfully. Now, she leaned back against a tree, folded her arms across her knees and buried her face in them. Then she sobbed as loudly and as long as Annie Smith had done.

Even if she had tried, she could not have avoided the comparison of herself to Kate and Annie, the two "traitors." Her own life of infidelity to her Lord, to his Church, and her deliberate, cowardly deception of her countrymen flooded her with shame and grief: *O God, forgive us all!*

When she emerged from the forest, Margaret saw Thompson across the pasture, leading John's horse to the stable. He was home! She ran the entire distance down the slope and across the pasture, nearly a quarter mile, scattering a cluster of ewes and lambs on her way, slamming shut the sheepgate behind her, and arriving completely breathless at the door, which was standing open. She collapsed against the doorpost to allow her heart to stop pounding and saw through the great portal from the hall to the drawing room her son standing by the banked fire. "John!" she breathed.

"Oh, Mother," he rushed toward her. "You should not run." He put his arm around her waist and led her to her chair to sit down. But Margaret saw, even in her breathless state, the shadow behind her son's warm brown eyes. Something was wrong. He would tell her, she knew, when she was breathing normally again.

"What is it, John? What has happened?" She forced her breath to slow down.

He sighed. "First, I know about what has happened in Kefington, so you don't have to be at pains to tell me." He dropped his voice to a whisper. "Let's take a walk in the garden when you've caught your breath." There was usually a servant close by, and even when there wasn't, Margaret and her children had made a habit of having private conversations only in certain places.

They were not, and had never been, recusants—not even before the pope finally excommunicated Elizabeth when she sent hundreds of whole families to the gallows in the north for rebelling against the suppression of their faith. Indeed, the persecution only intensified, so that now it was high treason to be in any kind of relationship with the Catholic Church, or even to aid those who were Catholic.

Ben Anders had been a man with more realistic foresight than most: he had known many years ago that the day would come when being a Catholic in England would be a crime against the state. The heavy fines for not attending services at the Church of England were not, he said, the end of the matter, but only the beginning. He was right. He and his family had attended the local "English church" regularly since the Act of Uniformity was passed in 1559. At every opportunity, they made confession to a priest, even as they knew they were confessing a deceit, if not an infidelity, that they would have to repeat. At times, the moral burden proved too much to bear—as it often did for Margaret.

Presently Margaret recovered her equilibrium, hastened by anxiety to know what John had to tell her. Hearing Eloise's footsteps in the hall, she rose and removed her cloak, slowly and deliberately. "Yes, I want to show you the buds on the new roses I planted in February. There are so many! I think this rose will be the best in the garden."

They walked unhurriedly through the hall and down the eastern wing of the house to the gallery overlooking the gardens on the south side, John's arm around his mother's waist. He could feel her trembling, and he wished he did not have to bear the heavy news he thought she was anticipating. They strolled down the gravel pathway to the rose garden, and Margaret bent over the new roses as John held her hand.

"Mother, Father Joseph has been taken. He was already at Manchester when I arrived there, but I did not find out about it until Mr. Lawson told me about a priest being held overnight in the jail while we were negotiating price on the spring shipment from Cumberland. Then I made inquiries as discreetly as I could. He is en route now to London—and the Tower."

"Oh!" Margaret straightened and clutched at her heart with one hand as she clung to her son's arm with the other. "Oh, no, no. Oh, John, has he any friends in London? Is there anything—anything at all—that we can do?"

"Mother, he was caught saying Mass, caught in the very act of 'high treason.' Do not hope, my dear. There is no remedy here."

Already overwhelmed with fear near to panic over not having heard from Eleanor, she began to sob, burying her face in her son's blue velvet doublet. He held her in his arms, knowing she would take this news hard after the Commission's visitation and the tragedy that had followed, but he did not know there had been no word from Eleanor. With his free hand, he reached into his mother's sleeve for her handkerchief, found it, and tried to hold it to her face. At length she took it from him, and he guided her along the few steps to a bench nearby.

Finally she spoke. "John, I've heard nothing from Eleanor."

"Oh, Mother, you know she does not always think to write."

"When I knew you had bad news, I was afraid—"

"You poor darling! No. I do not think I could have borne such news myself."

"But, John, just listen. Each time we go to Mass, I go to confession first with Father Joseph. Now he is no longer here—*O God, be merciful to him*—and I will tell you now what I must always confess by telling you this: I wept with relief just now—with *relief*, John—that it was Father Joseph and not Eleanor. But he is not here, will never be here again, and I cannot confess my sin." She wept anew, but softly this time, silently.

"Ah, Mother—and what would he do? He would absolve you, my dear. How can you *not* feel relieved that there is no evil news of her?" He held her head to his shoulder, gently stroking her neck under her muslin cap. "Father Joseph is so old, over seventy, I think. Let us pray that he does not survive the journey. He is very frail. And be at peace, Mother. God forgives you."

She squeezed his hand, thinking again how its strength so resembled Ben's. "I know that he has always forgiven me this sin. But I wonder: without confession, would I feel conviction? And without conviction, when would I stop *needing* forgiveness? Very soon, I think, very soon."

Then she told him the gruesome details of the visitation, Kate's execution, and finally of her visit to Annie Smith. "I am so thankful that Eleanor wasn't home. You know how she is. But shouldn't there have been some warning? Thompson usually knows about things before they happen."

"I asked him that question in the stable just now—why no one knew the queen's bishops were coming. He said he didn't know but thinks someone along the communication line must have been arrested. The net draws ever tighter. Walsingham's spies are everywhere now."

Margaret dabbed her eyes and pushed her handkerchief back into her sleeve. "I know it's better if Eleanor doesn't tell us exactly where she's going; still, I wish I knew. I so wish she would send word that she has arrived safely—wherever she went—and when she'll return."

The gravel path crunched under Eloise's running footsteps from the gallery. They stood. "She probably needs to know about dinner," said Margaret. "We didn't know you would be home, and all I asked for was the soup left from yesterday. Will that do? There should be fresh bread."

But Eloise was waving a letter in her hand. "Ma'am! You have a letter. I think it's from Mistress Eleanor!"

* * *

Later that afternoon, John was in his study, where he had been since dinner. His writing table was strewn with inkpots, sharpened quills, many books with figures and records of business transactions — investments, reports from his agents, correspondence. He did not pause when his man Richard came in to light the candles, did not look up, or seem to notice Richard's entrance or exit. John had an unusual ability to concentrate. And he had a talent for business, just as his father had before him.

He was only sixteen when his father died, too young to assume control of the vast and far-flung Anders holdings, even if Margaret had been willing to allow him to return from Oxford. They had been fortunate in having her brother, William Nelson, to look after their affairs until John could return and take over. Uncle William was a very successful wool merchant in York, and though he had other investments as well, he was not familiar with the barges Ben Anders owned on the Severn. He was cautious and astute, however, and he kept a running correspondence with John so that when he returned, he was able to take over smoothly, already familiar with the state of the Anders affairs through his uncle's correspondence. Now he entered in the current ledger the recent payment for wool that his agent had purchased in distant Cumberland and sold in Manchester, then laid his pen down, contented. His father would have been pleased.

He stood, stretched his long body, and flexed his fingers, cramped by much writing. He crossed the room to the large window that looked down on Margaret's garden. There she was, among her new roses, spading manure, with her skirts pinned up, her hair wrapped in a kerchief and topped by the flat cap that peasant women wore in the fields. He smiled. Would his mother be surprised to learn that she was probably the richest woman in western England? Yes—surprised, but not really interested. She cared for nothing but her children and the land. No, he decided, remembering her visit that day to Annie Smith, that wasn't all. She cared deeply for all the people who lived there, including those in the village. He raised his eyes to the silver-green hills. She was like those hills; perhaps they were even part of each other. The simplicity and strength of his mother's heart had made his own life, and the lives of everyone around her, simple and good. Business was complex and often difficult, politics even more so, but no part of the outside world ever touched the peace of Andersgate, protected not only by the remoteness of the region and by its situation within that region, but also by the spirit of his mother, which seemed to suffuse even the ancient forest and the hills.

When John was a child, he took his mother's strength for granted, but when he became a man, he learned its uniqueness and knew how blessed he and Eleanor had been in their mother—everyone around her benefited from that strength, that capacity for love and caring. As a man, he knew too that the source of that strength was her faith. It was because of his mother that John sometimes thought faith must be the most powerful force in the world—more powerful than business, politics, wars, or empires. No matter what those in temporary possession of power might believe, it was faith that wrote the world's history. And he knew too well that his own faith was weak, yet he believed devoutly in his mother's. He thought of Mary in London and decided that perhaps even Mary was an answer to his mother's prayers for him. She rarely mentioned it, but he knew she wanted him to find a good wife. It was time to tell his mother about Mary. He had hesitated until he was sure, but he decided then to tell her as soon as Eleanor returned. It was time for Mary to visit Andersgate.

But then, as he watched his mother, his smile faded. He remembered her at dinner reading Eleanor's letter aloud a second time. She was so relieved to receive the letter that she seemed to have forgotten Father Joseph for the moment. "John, I do wish she'd mentioned where she is. What do you suppose she means by this: 'I shall have an extra companion, newly arrived, for a part of my return journey. He is to stop somewhere in the Cotswolds, I think.' Now who do you suppose that is? Well, she cannot be away for very much longer. This was written four days ago."

A sudden coldness crept around John's heart. Why hadn't he thought of this before? "Newly arrived" could only mean a priest, and there was no more dangerous traveling companion than a priest. Eleanor had always conveyed messages—nothing more. He found himself as concerned as his mother had been before she received Eleanor's letter. He had to speak to Thompson—he had to have more information right away.

He went first to the stable, but the stableman told him that Mr. Thompson had gone "into his house." The servants never referred to the old steward's mysterious quarters merely as his office, but with some deference, as "Mr. Thompson's house." No one was allowed to go there except the family. The house was beyond Margaret's rose garden, its side entrance separated from the garden by a gated hedge. John did not want to encounter his mother in his present state of worry, so he circumvented her gardens by walking several hundred yards out of the way, going by the rear side of the dairy to the front entrance of the house. Thompson had installed several delaying locks, the first of which was a lock on the gate of the high, hedged fence that surrounded it. John rang the bell that hung beside it and waited for his steward to appear. After a moment, Thompson opened the little window in the gate, and seeing his master, he took the massive ring of keys from his belt and unlocked the gate.

"A word with you, Mr. Thompson."

"Yes, sir."

Neither spoke further until they arrived in the front room of the house that served as Thompson's office. In sharp contrast to John's study in the main house, Thompson's office was very tidy. A large table against the wall held many neat stacks of papers, bound in leather and arranged according to account. Underneath the table were two wooden chests containing the same accounts arranged by year in neat rows. If John had ever wanted to know the cost of farm implements to Andersgate two years ago, he would only have to ask Thompson. He would be able to hand him a yearly summary in minutes. He had often admired the efficiency of his steward. As it was, he depended on Richard, who acted as both secretary and personal servant, to keep his own records intelligibly organized.

He leaned against the writing table, which stood beneath the front window facing the gate, folded his arms, and crossed one white-hosed ankle over the other. He tried to maintain casualness in his posture in a rather too obvious attempt to be casual in his question.

"I know you've heard that Mother has finally received a letter from Eleanor. In it, she says she is to have a newly arrived traveling companion on her return. Do you know anything about that?"

"Yes. A little. There's a new young priest named Stephen Long, who was due to arrive at Devon. I expect Miss Eleanor was sent to meet him."

"I see. So she is in Devon?"

"Well, that wasn't to be her destination, exactly."

"No? Then why is she there?"

"John—"

"I know. I know it's best that I not have information I do not actually have need of." So Eleanor had indeed met an arriving priest and would travel with him. His anxiety grew.

Thompson shifted his feet. "Ordinarily, that's true, but if there is some reason—"

"Well, actually, yes, though the reason is not a valid one, I admit. It's just that, after what's happened to Father Joseph—"

"Yes, I know. And by the way, I may as well tell you that since he was the only priest we had in this part of the country, it may be that this new priest will replace him here instead of stopping in Warwick, as planned. He has to go to Bath and speak to Father Farwell first, in any event. But I expect he will be sent hereabouts. We'll have to wait until Eleanor returns to find out."

"Well, that is, in fact, the concern. Mother is feeling relieved because she's got this letter, but it was written four days ago, Thompson—four days. *Where is she?*"

Thompson hesitated. He had known John all his life. Apart from the familiarity of lifelong close acquaintance, there was also the unique relationship of John's necessary deference to Thompson for information on certain matters. Thompson was the hub of a wheel, as it were, of underground communication among Catholics, a position that not only made him the recipient of information, but also the one to decide who needed to know which parts and to delegate messengers accordingly. John's sister, Eleanor, was one of those messengers. Thompson had been at Andersgate since before John's birth, a part of the family, and especially in private, there was no distinction between master and servant. The two men stood on equal footing, but on the topic of conversation now, Thompson himself was actually the master.

"I know you're worried, John. She wasn't supposed to go to Devon, but only to Bath—two days, maybe a few more if Father Farwell sent her somewhere else. When I learned about the new priest, I suspected she might have been sent on to Devon to meet him and perhaps to take him back to Father Farwell there in Bath. That is what I believe has happened, and of course, that would make her journey much longer. It is likely that she's on her way to Bath now with the new priest. She should be back in a day or two."

"Well, I shall be honest about this. If I had known she had a mission that dangerous, I would have forbade her going — though I don't suppose that would have done any good."

Thompson made a little smile. He knew Eleanor's stubborn self-will very well. For just a moment he had the wistful expression common to the old, remembering fond images of the past. He had taught Eleanor to ride at her insistence when she was only seven, and he remembered her now, stamping her little foot next to her pony when he told her she'd have to ride sidesaddle, like a lady. "I will not!" she sputtered. "That is just too silly!" Eventually she had had to learn sidesaddle, of course, but it was a fight all the way.

Thompson placed his hand on John's arm. "I hope you know that I would never have sent her on such a mission — no matter how much she argued. It had to be Father Farwell, and he wouldn't have done it either if there had been anyone else able to go."

John sighed. "Yes, I do know that. But now, none of us will breathe easy until she returns, with or without the priest."

But Thompson was more worried than he had revealed, much more. The information he had given John was really only speculation, unconfirmed by any communication from Father Farwell in Bath. Actually, that lack of communication from Bath was the basis of his hope, because he knew that Father Farwell would inform the family immediately if anything had happened to Eleanor — and so far, he'd received no message from him. But his eyes kept straying toward the road from the east, where Sam, Father Farwell's messenger, might appear any time now.

3

The next morning, May 22, in Blexton

Patricia Wilson sat across the dining table from her husband at the rectory of St. Anselm's. She watched him while he ate his breakfast of salted cod, bacon, brown bread, and cheese. She herself never ate before dinner, but she always sat with him while he ate his breakfast because she believed that a wife should provide companionship to her husband at his meals. She watched him wipe bits of bacon and grease from his mouth with the back of his hand. His oily gray curls spilled forward beside his long pale face as he leaned slightly forward to cut the fish with his knife. Patricia could not remember a time when the deep vertical creases between his brows were not there, brows which were, she observed again, wiry, gray, as unkempt as the rest of his person. His cheeks sagged down into his bearded jowls. She watched his fingers as he ate; the nails were never completely clean. Every morning she tried not to see these things, tried to find something more pleasing to observe, but it seemed the harder she tried, the more revulsion she felt.

As closely as she watched him, he never looked at her. In fact, it was Andrew Wilson's habit to ignore his wife completely unless she spoke to him, and she catalogued this habit somewhere between his morning odor and the smear of grease on his beard. She fingered the immaculate small white ruff at her neck, then examined her hands. It was better to think of someone else, something else, anything else. So Caroline Wingate is barren, she thought. A small smile almost broke the hard line of her mouth. Captain Wingate would certainly find that situation unacceptable, she decided. And apparently he'd been troubled enough about it to consult Beryl, of all people. She sniffed. Beryl's scrawled note had been almost illegible, but at least she could write. No one in the parish knew that Beryl was her third cousin on her mother's side from Blakely Down—and they never would, if she could help it. And then another thought caused the smile actually to surface, an event rare enough to cause the reverend to look up at her sharply for a moment. She caught herself, however, and resumed her studious examination of her fingernails. It was too funny: the captain thought a woman had to enjoy herself in bed in order to conceive a child. The dear! And now an even stranger occurrence broke her husband's concentration on his cod—a look of actual tenderness settled on her face. And this expression was superseded by a look of mounting interior glee: Caroline was cold to him in bed! Who could believe it? The news was worth much more than half a crown. She would enjoy it all day—and who knew? Maybe Captain Wingate might call on Andrew, might need some advice about divorcing his wife.

"My dear," asked the reverend, "are you quite all right?"

"Of course, Andrew. I just remembered an amusing story Betty told me this morning."

It seemed extraordinary to Andrew that the housemaid would tell any sort of story to his wife at all, let alone an amusing one. He resumed his silent focus on his breakfast. No, no story. She was likely remembering some young man looking at her admiringly. Only something like that would have made his wife smile. "Will you be visiting the sick today?" he asked her, noticing that she was dressed rather well in her green damask.

"Yes. I shall be leaving when you've done with your breakfast—unless you need anything before I go?"

"Will you be visiting the Braithlows?"

"Andrew, I really do not think that is appropriate."

"You know very well that Mrs. Braithlow is quite ill, and even though they are recusants, they are members of this parish. I will not have them treated badly. I insist that you include Mrs Braithlow among your calls, and I insist that you behave courteously when you call on her." He did not want to argue with his wife on this subject again. He knew that her refusal to accord recusants the courtesy that was due to them was not a consequence of any religious scruple, nor of any loyalty to the queen, though she claimed both. No. Almost all of his wife's actions were motivated by simple snobbery.

"I will obey you in this, Andrew, but I must express my own opinion that it is quite inappropriate for the parson's wife to call on papists."

"I will not argue this matter." He rose, dusting crumbs from his lap. "I will be in my study until dinner. If you return before that time, please visit me there and tell me how you found Mrs. Braithlow. Otherwise, I shall see you at dinner and will expect your report at that time."

He left the room, and moments later, Patricia heard the door of his study close quietly. She sat for some moments in silence while Betty cleared the dishes from the table, her expression having resettled into its customary rigidity. But for that expression, she might have been a beautiful woman. She was more than twenty years younger than her husband. People often called her handsome. She had a fine figure, a straight carriage, with a cultivated elegance in her bearing. Her black hair was piled high and always dressed; but her mouth was set in a hard line, and her black eyes had a startling piercing quality that people often found unnerving. That piercing look intensified when she was angry—as she now was. Andrew might live to regret that false charity, she reflected, and perhaps sooner rather than later, now that the queen had a new militia, established purposely to deal with just such people as the Braithlows—well, those who hid popish priests anyway.

Andrew closed the door with a sigh of relief. Patricia was a trial, a daily one, and his study was his escape from that trial. Not that the Braithlows, and other recusants, were not also a trial, though of quite a different sort. He worried that the new militia would cause trouble for the recusants in his parish, perhaps very serious trouble, and he wished they would not be so outspoken. More, he wished they would do as he had done—hold their peace and be patient.

Those like himself who had been Catholic priests during Queen Mary's reign had been forced to sign the Oath of Supremacy acknowledging Queen Elizabeth as head of the Church—just as those had done who suffered under the Protestant advisers of the young King Edward during his reign before Queen Mary ascended the throne. It was all just politics, ever changing, and not reason enough to risk one's fortune, let alone one's life. Monarchs come and go, after all, but the Church established by Christ himself would remain. No law of any government was going to change that. Elizabeth might change her mind about Catholics at any time, he often told himself, though he knew well that such an event would never happen because of the Catholic Mary Stuart's rightful claim to the throne; Elizabeth's security was contingent on outlawing Catholics.

But he also wished the High Commission would be satisfied with the fines charged against the recusants for not attending his services. The fines had impoverished several families who once were very prosperous; some had found it necessary to sell most of their property to pay them, and some who were even less able to pay had lost everything, become vagrants, and were thus imprisoned for that crime as well as the crime of being Catholics.

Why were they so stubborn? He frowned, reflecting on the recusants' obstinacy. Were they saints? He wondered often about that. But each time he wondered, he answered his own question: No, they were not saints, merely imprudent zealots. But if the question had already been answered so many times, why did he keep asking it? He decided that it was because of his concern for them, his compassion, his desire to protect them. Indeed, it was true that part of him wanted very much for them to stop hurting themselves, to be more careful. Having often thought about it, he knew that part very well. Yet, there was another part of him that wanted them to continue, even to the death. He never thought about that part. It would have been imprudent.

He unlocked the cabinet that held his private collection of books and took down from the shelf his new volume of commentary on Irenaeus, recently arrived from his friend in Rome, and settled himself in his chair by the window. Latin in church was outlawed, but he had a great many works in Latin and Greek, none of them written by members of the Church of England. His library, he had often thought with a small measure of self-approval, was his own recusancy. But on this morning, he avoided that kind of reflection, which usually served to improve his mood. After the exchange with Patricia, he felt vulnerable. The commentary would help.

Reverend Wilson was a good pastor; he had often been told so. But he believed that anyone could be a good "pastor" who had a charitable nature and the position that allowed it. Indeed, he had met men—and women—who were better pastors than he was, people who were not even particularly Christian, just the kind of people who were understanding or sympathetic. Being a pastor was a clerical garment he wore, and he wore it well. But when he was alone, in his heart, he knew he was simply a scholar; he knew that he was meant to be enclosed in a monastery somewhere, contentedly celibate, contentedly praying, reading, and writing. He had missed the opportunity to be what he truly was. It was just that he could not bear to think of these things, not just now—not anytime, really.

There was a soft tapping at his door. Betty opened it just far enough to speak to him. "Sir, Sheriff Marley and Captain Wingate are in the hall. They would like a word with you."

He replaced the commentary on the shelf, somewhat puzzled by this visit. Marley might call on him if there had been an accident or some emergency requiring the parson, but what did Wingate want? If anything had happened to one of the servants at his house, he would not have come personally. He hoped nothing was wrong with Mrs. Wingate. Too bad, he thought, that Patricia had left for her rounds. She would be bitterly disappointed to miss a call from the handsome young captain. "Make them comfortable in the drawing room, Betty, and tell them I shall be there presently."

"Yes, sir." She closed the door softly.

Andrew went to the small mirror over the bureau and smoothed his hair, looked down at his tunic to make sure he was presentable, hesitated and then decided that his felt slippers were acceptable. As always, he closed and locked the doors of the cabinet that housed his collection of Catholic scholarly works before leaving the room.

Sheriff Marley and Captain Wingate had not gone into the small drawing room but were still standing in the anteroom. Andrew judged that whatever their business was, they didn't think it warranted discussion. "Good morning, gentlemen. What may I do for you? Please come in and sit down."

Robert answered. "Good morning, sir. We are sorry to intrude on you, to call unannounced this way, and we will not come inside to disturb you further. Our business is brief but necessary. I must first explain to you why Captain Wingate accompanies me here. The captain has been made magistrate by special appointment of the queen's council. Unfortunately, our business here involves his authority."

"I see. My congratulations, Captain, on your appointment." He looked appraisingly at Edward for a moment, wondering what the appointment really meant—not so much for Edward, but for others. "What is the nature of this business?"

Edward spoke for the first time as Magistrate. It occurred to him even as he spoke that the "authority" was not really his own, but Robert's. He perceived fleetingly, like a little flash of light, that his role here was simply to legitimize Robert's decisions, not his own. Nevertheless, he felt some gratification by the rector's appraising congratulations, some new sense of importance, and the feeling was a very pleasant one. "Thank you, Reverend. I think Sheriff Marley could explain what has happened better than I, and why we request your assistance in this sad business."

Robert rose to the assignment: "There is a farmer named Leacham a few miles east—perhaps you know him, sir?—who sits now in jail. He came upon a group of papists having a meeting—I do not think it was a Mass, just a meeting, a prayer meeting, perhaps—in his barn on the night before last. Now, Leacham tells me, and perhaps he's speaking truthfully—you may know him better than I—that he was so enraged by the treachery of his own plowman—the plowman was among them—that he stole back into his house and got his wheel-lock, returned to the barn, and shot them dead."

"What a tragedy! Yes," Andrew said, "I do know Leacham, and yes, he is a very hot-headed man. How did he know them to be papists?"

"He said they were doing that Latin mummery with beads."

"Ah," replied Andrew. He paused and sighed. "Well, the plowman may have deceived him, but that hardly justifies Farmer Leacham's reaction, so I'm not surprised he's in jail. But what do you now require of me, sirs?"

Robert answered, "Well, I have acquainted Captain Wingate here with all the details and turned the matter over to him for his judgment. I must say, sir, that I believe we are fortunate to have such a wise and compassionate magistrate among us. He has decided that since the militia may have arrested the papists anyway, possibly under suspicion of meeting in order to plan aid to a popish priest—an arrest, I may say, sir, that would have done the reputation of our village and our law-abiding citizens no good—perhaps clemency may be called for, under those circumstances, in prosecuting the overzealous farmer, though he should be given very stern warning against such rash action in the future." Robert paused, watching the reverend's face. "The trouble is, sir, the bodies."

"Hmm, yes, I see. How many?"

Edward was as relieved as Robert to see that the reverend was not going to question their judgment. "Three," Robert answered. "Only the plowman is known. John Taversley, his name was. No family around here. The other two, a woman and a youth, are not known to me or to Leacham. I believe they must be strangers here, though they do not appear to be foreign. The woman looks to be gentry by her dress, and the youth may have been her servant. I think, and have so suggested to the Captain, that the bodies should be burnt. We have come to ask your opinion on this plan, and perhaps your prayers over them, for they cannot be buried in the churchyard." He did not mention that he and Edward thought the parson's prayers would lend respectability to their actions.

"Why not?"

"Well, sir, they were papists. Traitors."

There was a long pause then, as though communication had suddenly gone awry.

"Sheriff, most of the graves in the churchyard are occupied by Catholics."

"Oh. Well, yes. Yes, sir, of course you're right—but these people are outlaws. And that is consecrated ground."

"And do you think we should dig up every grave and burn the remains?"

Robert was flustered, embarrassed. He had not had to deal with the mere day-to-day confusion that resulted from the view of Catholics as outlaws. "Well, of course not. If you think it is all right to bury—"

"I most certainly do."

"Yes, sir. Well, then, perhaps you will say some prayers over the bodies before their burial?"

"Of course."

Edward cleared his throat. "Very good of you, Reverend Wilson. If you will get word to the gravediggers, I will accompany the sheriff to the Leacham farm." He did not mention that Robert would first release Leacham from jail in exchange for his promise not to mention the two escapees. "We will have the bodies brought by cart to the graveyard by late afternoon, surely before dusk—do you think so, sheriff?"

"Yes, Captain. The farm's only six miles out. But there is no need for you to go too, if you would rather not."

"Indeed I would rather not," replied Edward, very glad to have an end to his involvement in the matter. "We appreciate your assistance, Reverend. I will return home now, but I think it is appropriate—is it not?—that I be present at the burial service? Please send someone to fetch me at that time."

"I will come for you, Captain," Robert offered. He turned to Reverend Wilson. "And I will call on you, Reverend, when I return with the cart."

"Very good, gentlemen," said Wilson. "Good day to you both." He closed the door gently behind them and walked back down the hallway to his study, feeling sickened by this turn of events. Leacham was a fool. "Patriotism" had given him an excuse for his hatred and violence. How many others were there like him, who used that same false patriotism as a self-righteous mask for their envy and hate—and their greed. He had always believed it was a mistake to reward informers by selling them confiscated Catholic properties at cheap prices—and now a murderer would be allowed to go free, unpunished. Marley and Wingate were both decent men, but he knew what their real motives were in granting "clemency" to Leacham.

Outside, Robert and Edward mounted their horses in silence. Both men were feeling some embarrassment over their proposal to burn the bodies at Leacham's farm. They had agreed not to mention the two escapees. Finally, Edward broke the silence with a comment on a different topic: "Thank you, Robert, for not insisting that I go to that farm. Caroline wants to visit her aunt in Somerset, and she wants to leave right away—tomorrow, in fact. There is much to do to prepare for her journey. I don't want her to have too little escort."

"Right. The roads are dangerous now. Indeed, Edward, there's no need for you to attend the reverend's prayers."

"Oh, I will be present. It seems appropriate for a magistrate, I think." He really had no idea whether it was appropriate or not.

The two men rode away in opposite directions. Edward went home, and Robert went to the jail to release Leacham. It seemed to Edward that all had gone well enough with his first judgment as magistrate, though he had been surprised by Reverend Wilson's chastisement of Robert for suggesting that the bodies be burnt. Of course, he was right. It had been their intention to get the reverend's sanction of their actions by asking him to say prayers at the farm before the burning. He felt relieved now that the suggestion had been put forth as Robert's, even though it had actually been his own idea. After all, when Catholics were convicted by the Council in London of practicing their faith, the punishment was much worse, especially for priests. There was always torture on the rack first, then hanging, but then they were cut down while still alive, drawn out on the executioner's table, castrated, and disemboweled. Then the bodies were quartered and the pieces placed on pikes at various places in London. It was the penalty for treason against Her Majesty.

Edward shuddered. This punishment was accomplished in the name of the queen. He had met Elizabeth once on the occasion of his commission after a successful raid on the coast of Spain, just after his marriage to Caroline three years ago. After he was presented, he rose from his deep bow to see a tall woman with wiry hair the color of withered carrots, and the coldest, hardest small eyes he had ever seen on anyone, man or woman. "I understand you are lately wed, Captain." Her voice sounded far away, as though she spoke from a mountaintop.

"Yes, Majesty." He was afraid to speak, afraid to move. He had the feeling that displeasing this person would be the worst fate that could befall anyone in the world.

She parted her thin red lips, revealing an uneven row of small yellow teeth. Her eyelids dropped, and her heavily powdered face became a suggestive leer. "Pity," she said, and her ladies who gathered around her tittered. His revulsion was so quick in his surprise that he could not counter it in time. Later, he prayed she had not seen it in his expression, yet he knew those small eyes saw everything around her and far beyond. He wanted never to be the object of her attention again; something told him that if he were, it would not be an expression of her favor but of her revenge. He hoped his appointment as magistrate had not been made with her knowledge. It was too frightening to think it had been her order.

He brushed such unpleasant thoughts from his mind and thought of Caroline instead. When he told her at breakfast about his new position as magistrate, her eyes became very round for a long moment. Then she asked him if he was pleased.

"Well, yes, my dear, I am. It is an honor, you know."

She smiled then. He loved her smile, and he was glad that it was somewhat rare. It was always a lovely surprise. "Then I am pleased also, Edward." Then she talked about her concern for her Aunt Margaret, mentioning the letter she had received from her, saying that Margaret was alone because both Eleanor and John were away, and ended by asking him if he would permit her to pay a visit to her aunt — a very brief visit, perhaps just a week; she would be away a fortnight at most. Edward was in a generous mood. It had been over eight months since Caroline had seen her family, and since the visit would be such a short one, he agreed. She would leave the following morning, taking only Joseph and her personal servant, Norma, with her. He frowned. Joseph alone was not enough protection; he would send Owen from the stables as well — and more, if he could arrange it on such short notice. He spurred his horse lightly; much preparation was indeed required, and he needed to be at home. He regretted now his offer to be present for the graveside prayers and decided he would decline when Robert called for him that afternoon. After all, Robert had already said his presence wasn't required.

* * *

Patricia had put off her visit to Mrs. Braithlow until last. Now, avoiding a return home early enough to meet Andrew's requirement of a report, she sat with her friend Mrs. Lewis, so indignant over not being received by Mrs. Braithlow that she could hardly speak. The two women sat eating sweetmeats in Mrs. Lewis's home on the outskirts of the village. She was trying to express her outrage, but each effort caused her to choke on her food.

"I ask you, madam, can you believe it?" she complained. "They make a public show of their utter disregard for Her Majesty's laws — *and* their disrespect for my dear husband — by not attending church — not even *once*. And then to —" She spluttered, unable to conclude her thought.

"Oh, my poor Mrs. Wilson. Now tell me again; what did the impudent maid say?"

"Oh, well, at first she said, 'Pardon, ma'am, I'll inquire' and left me standing there outside — standing outside, mind you! — while she went to ask the wretched woman if she'd receive me. Then — and I mean it was ever so long I was left standing there — she returned and said, 'Mrs. Braithlow says she's sorry, ma'am, but she's too ill for a visit.' Now, you *know*, Mrs. Lewis, you just know, she was no such thing. She just wanted to take advantage of my call as an opportunity for offense."

"Of course she did." Mrs. Lewis patted Patricia's hand and passed the tray of sweetmeats to her again. "She has no shame, you know. But I'm so sorry you had to suffer this outrage, my dear. And then what happened?"

"Well, she just closed the door. I mean, I had not yet turned away and the vicious thing simply closed the door right in my face. I was so mortified I nearly fainted — nearly fainted, I tell you. I believe I would have done so if the young Braithlow boy had not come round the house at that moment and caught me as I swayed backward."

"Oh, my goodness. Now, there's a wonder. How do such people manage to raise a well-mannered boy, I ask you," clucked Mrs. Lewis.

"It's as my dear husband so often does say, Mrs. Lewis: The ways of the Lord are mysterious."

"Indeed they are, Mrs. Wilson, indeed they are."

"I mean, really. Now here is my dear husband — he's so kind, you know — can't help himself — it's just his nature. Mrs. Lewis, I must say that I am truly blessed to be married to such a good man, a holy man if ever there was one. I did not want to call on

Mrs. Braithlow, but Andrew would insist. He's never mindful of himself, only of others. That's my Andrew." She dabbed at the corners of her eyes with a handkerchief, apparently overcome by thoughts of her husband's kindness.

"Well, Mrs. Wilson, I must say that I believe your husband to be equally blessed. How many wives—even of pastors—would subject themselves to such humiliation out of regard for their husband's wishes? I just ask you." Mrs. Lewis called for more sweetmeats.

"Mrs. Lewis, I'll tell you plainly. I just try to be worthy of my position. Do you understand? After all, I am the wife of a man with a high calling. But I can tell you: it is not easy, Mrs. Lewis, it is not easy to hold such a position."

And so it went. By the time Patricia left the home of her friend, she knew she would arrive at her own home too late for dinner, a situation for which she felt very grateful, since she would not have to submit to Andrew's questions. With any luck, by the time she saw him at supper, he might even have forgotten his commandment that she visit the Braithlows.

Meanwhile, at Somerfield, Caroline sat on the side of her bed and observed Norma's fussing about with the packing. The maid was excited to be going on a journey with her mistress, and Caroline enjoyed her excitement, though she had to stop Norma from packing too many dresses, gloves, shoes, and headpieces.

"Norma, please—remember that we'll be at Andersgate for only a week. And my aunt does not have fancy supper parties for all those dresses you want to pack. You've been there before, and you know how plainly they live. I'll wear the green silk for travel—then just one or two plain woolens and that simple white coif, and perhaps one dress for their church on Sunday."

"But, my lady, suppose they have guests you don't know about now?"

"That's very unlikely. Remember we are taking only two packhorses. Would you load the poor beasts down so much they can't walk?"

"We should take a third, do you not think so? After all, I must have a change of clothes as well."

"Pray take only one change, Norma. Believe me, there will be no occasion for more." Caroline knew that Norma had visions of festive supper parties, many guests who would need to be impressed by the finery of her mistress, but most of all, she knew Norma wanted to impress the servants at Andersgate with her own importance as the personal maid of such a "fine lady" as Caroline.

Norma sighed, reluctantly letting go of her imaginary fancy-dress festivities. It was true: Mrs. Wingate's family lived almost as plainly as ordinary manor folk—though she knew them to be very wealthy.

"Ma'am, would you like me to pack your personal things in the little satchel?" she asked.

"No, I'll do that later. Don't forget the stout boots for walking, though. My aunt loves to go walking in the woods." Caroline always packed her own small bag because she took her rosary and her prayer book. She thought happily of walking with Margaret through the forest that separated Andersgate from the village of Kefington on the Severn. None of the local folk ever ventured into the forest because it was very dense and ancient; they believed it to be filled with packs of wild boar and other dangerous beasts, but she and her cousins had played in the forest as children and never once had they seen even a serpent to cause them fear. Remembering those happy times, she almost forgot the real reason for her visit now—the fear she had sensed in her aunt's letter. But perhaps, she thought hopefully, I am wrong. And perhaps Eleanor and John would have returned by the time she arrived. And perhaps, even, John will tell Aunt

Margaret about Mary Posten. She hoped he would do so while she was there. He had written her about Mary; Eleanor knew also—even Thompson knew—but John had been reluctant to tell his mother because he knew she would be only too ready to have him married, and he wanted to be sure first. It would make her Aunt Margaret so happy to know that John had found the woman who would be his wife.

But then just the thought of "wife" made her realize that Edward would want her tonight especially, the night before her departure. She fought back an instinctive dread, then begged forgiveness for it. Edward was so patient, so kind—how she wished she had the same feeling for him as he had for her. The weight of her guilt in failing to make her husband happy settled over her again; it was never absent for long. She would have to confess it again to Father Joseph at Andersgate, and she dreaded that too. His counsel was always the same: She should think of how good her husband was, how fortunate she was to have a husband who loved her—but that counsel did not cause her to desire her husband. Instead, it only made the guilt harder to bear.

* * *

Late that afternoon at the Leacham farm, Robert waited for Mrs. Leacham to bring linen from the house to cover the bodies. Simon and one of his workers would roll the bodies in the sheets, then lift them into the cart. Robert stared down at the bodies. Taversley was lying about four feet from the other two, face down. A large black span of dried blood splayed outward from the middle of his coarse brown tunic; he had been shot from behind. The well-dressed woman was lying halfway on her side, her skirts askew, revealing white underskirts beneath the blue satin. She had been shot in the chest. The young man, in brown breeches and an oiled leather jerkin, lay across her body. He had evidently tried to shield her body with his own. Robert thought he couldn't be more than sixteen, very young to die a hero's death. He sighed and leaned over the woman's face in an effort to see her more clearly. He drew his breath in sharply. The woman looked so like Caroline Wingate — the same brown curls, pointed small chin, and cream-white skin. The resemblance was striking.

Mrs. Leacham brought the bedsheets. Her face was sullen. "I do say, my lord sheriff, this is a dear price. These sheets will leave us short in the house. I don't see no reason the traitors couldn't just be burnt here instead."

Simon Leacham noted the stern look on Robert's face and hastened to soften his wife's complaint. "Now, Lettie, it is small price to pay for your man's freedom, is it not? Your man is home, and all you're out is three sheets? Come now." Very much to his surprise, Farmer Leacham had been subjected to a whipping by the sheriff, not with a whip but with words. Robert had told him he was free to go, thanks only to the mercy of the magistrate, but that if he ever took the law into his own hands again, he'd pay full price for it, magistrate or no, by hanging.

Leacham had protested: "But they were doing treason right there in my own barn, my lord sheriff—on my own property! I'm a freeholder, I am. That's *my* land."

But Robert bellowed at him: "I don't care whose land it is, you stupid man, you can't commit murder on it. What are you doing with a wheel-lock pistol, anyway? I couldn't afford such as that; I daresay even Sir Arnold couldn't."

Leacham knew he had better back down. The conversation was going places he did not want to go. He'd got the pistol from a militia man in a game of chance at The Three Lions. He allowed himself to appear duly chastised, even if his heart was not in it.

His wife caught his warning eye then. "Oh, aye, that it is," she replied, "a small price for my Simon's freedom. Yes, sir, it is."

She shook out the three sheets one at a time and handed them to her husband. Leacham and his helper stood at the head and foot of Taversley's body to lift him into one of them. The bodies were lifted onto the three sheets, but before they rolled them up, Mrs. Leacham spotted the rosaries. Taversley's rosary lay about two feet from his outstretched arm, made of small square pieces of wood—homemade, perhaps. But the woman's rosary was made of pearls and gemstones. She picked up the wooden rosary and dropped it on Taversley's body, but when she picked up the woman's rosary, she hesitated.

"Lettie, you just drop that thing right on top of her. It's the devil's own plaything, it is, no matter how pretty you might think it."

She reluctantly dropped the rosary on the woman's body, and the bodies were rolled up in their sheets and loaded onto the cart. Leacham climbed onto the cart behind his horse as Robert mounted his own horse. He knew he would not mention to Edward the woman's resemblance to Caroline, and he briefly wondered why. But the answer that came was a little troubling, so he decided to forget about it.

* * *

Dusk in Devonshire found Reverend Wilson in the church-yard, standing at the head of an open unmarked grave containing three shrouded bodies. Only the gravediggers were present, along with Sheriff Marley. He read aloud the Twenty-Third Psalm: "Yea, though I walk through the valley of the shadow of death …" Robert was surprised to hear the reverend's voice break.

4

The following day, May 23, on the road to Bath

Stephen reached down and patted Stella's neck. The mare was
not young, and she had already made one trip to Bath and back
to Blexton when Francis Braithlow rode to Father Farwell's
house in Bath to tell him the sad news of the murder of three
Catholics in Devonshire. Father Farwell would have the awful
task of informing the families of the slain. Now that there were
no Catholic bishops in England, the elderly priest, who could
no longer ride, functioned as bishop for southwestern England.
It was Father Farwell who had sent the young woman and her
escort to bring Stephen to his house in Bath, but Josiah Braithlow had met him at the top of the cliff path instead. Then Josiah
had taken him to The Three Lions, where Stephen had originally planned to meet his escort, and given him food and drink
there before taking him home to his farm.

Josiah's son, Francis Braithlow, along with his younger
brother Philip, had escaped the slaughter in Leacham's barn,
and he had already departed for Bath to inform Father Farwell
of the murders of the escorts by the time Stephen arrived at the
farm. In a village as small and insular as Blexton, Stephen's presence put the family at serious risk. They were known Catholics,
but not guilty of any crime except recusancy; harboring a priest,
however, was a capital offense. That was the reason none of the
local Catholics had been assigned to meet him. After some discussion about what to do, it was decided that Stephen would

travel on alone to Bath as soon as Francis returned with the horse.

When he returned, Francis gave him detailed directions to Father Farwell's house. Among other duties, Father Farwell assigned priests to various parts of southwestern England. Because Stephen was from a small village only twenty miles north of Bath, he hoped to be assigned somewhere in that area. His family still lived in that village, and he knew they were expecting him.

Stella had had some rest before Stephen departed, and she seemed to be enjoying the exercise, but Stephen felt that a slower pace might be better for her. Besides, there was no need to hurry. He would stay at an inn called The Rose and Thorn tonight and arrive at Father Farwell's house after leisurely travel tomorrow, following the careful directions Francis had given him. He had said Mass in the Braithlows' barn before his departure, for the souls of the victims, and in thanksgiving for the escape of the Braithlows' sons from the shooting, and, as always, for the safety of all the faithful in England.

For all the faithful in England. The phrase, ever in his heart when not on his lips, caused his spirit to mourn so deep within him that he was not even able to articulate his prayer. Indeed, he could never bring all the faithful in England to his consciousness. It was a prayer too immense to be held even in his thought, let alone in any prayer he might feebly utter. Instead, he thought always of persons, not people—of his family; of friends he had grown up with; of his classmates at Oxford, so many of them secret Catholics; and of his teachers and fellow seminarians at Douai in France—persons always, faces, voices, like the French oarsmen whose names he didn't even know, who had rowed the small boat to the Devonshire coast from the ship anchored several miles out at sea, risking their lives so that the English might have another priest among them. He was overwhelmed by his unworthiness of the risks so many took, the sacrifices so many had made for his priesthood.

And their kindness, their simple goodness. Mrs. Braithlow thought his hosen should be washed clean of salt and sand. Because she was too ill to do it herself, the younger son—he was about fifteen—had done it for her. Josiah had taken him to the alehouse to eat because Mrs. Braithlow was too ill to cook, and the maid, the only servant at the farm, could not know of his presence there. And he knew well that they had packed their best food for his journey. *Make me worthy, Lord*, he prayed, as "all the faithful in England" seemed to rise up like the waves of a vast sea, submerging him, drowning him. He consciously dismissed them all, reflecting again, as he had often done before, that love was a burden too great for his small human heart to bear. He thought it ironic that he could function as a priest for them only if he chose not to feel the love he had for them. If he let himself feel that love, it would paralyze him, consume and destroy him.

There was a time—was it really only a few generations ago?—when the most serious question a young man considering the priesthood might ask himself was whether he could forego a wife and family in order to take the Church for his bride. Stephen was concerned sometimes that his own answer to this question might have been made too easily. He had never felt a deep desire for a family of his own. When he entered the seminary, he had assumed that the decision to live a celibate life would be much more difficult than the consequent decision to forego marriage. After all, chastity was required of all the faithful, but celibacy was another matter altogether. To be chaste in marriage meant only fidelity to one's wife, but to be chaste as a priest meant celibacy. He had learned to live with it the same way most other seminarians had done—to realize that it was, like everything else in life, a choice, one that sometimes must be made daily—a choice between keeping his vow and breaking it. So far, the cost of keeping the vow was not as great as the cost of breaking it would have been—that was a cost too painful even to imagine.

But what had surprised him in seminary was that the other young candidates for the priesthood felt that marriage—not celibacy itself—was the greater sacrifice. One young Englishman had left the seminary, unable to forget the woman he had loved, even though she had married someone else. The woman still reigned in his heart, married or not. She was lost to him forever, but he could not be a priest. Stephen had never been in love, had never made the sacrifice that so many of his fellow seminarians had made. And not having had that experience, it surprised him to find that they held marriage and family to be the greater sacrifice; Stephen thought celibacy would be more difficult. In Scripture, Christ said that they would be blessed who would do as he had done, who would "make themselves eunuchs for the sake of the kingdom of Heaven." And that had been Stephen's choice.

But that question was in the past anyway. Now, in this time of persecution, that was not the question young men had to ask themselves. Fear flooded his mind again. *What was he doing?* He loved life; he did not want to die; especially he did not want to die the agonizing death that the queen reserved for captured priests. Was it too late? Yes, too late. His vows were made, he was ordained. Could he run away from his priesthood? Yes, but he knew he never would. *Why was he doing this?* But again, as always, he could not answer himself. He could only pray, "God help me, I do not know why."

Then he smiled as he ran his fingers through the horse's mane. Even Stella was doing her part for him. He could tell she wanted to move faster, and though he knew the road ahead was long, he gave in to her desire and broke the horse's slow trot to a canter—past the blackberry bushes covered now in white blossoms, past dark hawthorn hedges, past wild apple trees with their small fruit just beginning to appear, and along green grasses made soft as down by frequent rain and fog, which made the rare sunlit morning in an English spring unspeakably glorious, the dew covering everything around him with a blanket of diamonds.

* * *

Caroline had resisted Edward's attempts to force still more armed escorts on her journey. She thought Owen and Joseph were really quite enough, though neither was very skilled in weaponry. That fact had made him want to send others, armed deputies from the constabulary, with her. She had been able to resist him in this attempt, but now she wondered if she had done wisely. Of her three companions, she actually had more faith in Norma than in either of the two men. She thought that young Owen would be a more competent defender than Joseph, not least because he did not brandish his pistol about as old Joseph did, but kept it tucked safely in his belt. But Norma, she thought, was a clever woman who had more common sense than either of the men—or herself, for that matter.

For now, just for now, she had decided to release her fear and all sorrowful thoughts. She would see Aunt Margaret again! And John and Eleanor as well, for surely they would both return before Caroline arrived—or perhaps Eleanor was already there; perhaps she'd arrived after Aunt Margaret wrote the letter to Caroline. She thrilled at the thought of attending Mass in old Thompson's house, seeing Father Joseph again, praying without fear with her family, and most of all, receiving Holy Communion. She felt a lightness in her spirit she had not known for months, like clouds lifting after many days of darkness and heaviness. Her life was unchanged, but for now, just for now, she was content with it.

The riders were traveling in single file on a narrow lane at the edge of a forest toward the road that went north to Bath, Joseph in front, then Norma, followed by Caroline, and Owen at the rear, with the reins of two packhorses. Twice they had passed travelers on foot, who moved aside and allowed their horses to pass. The travelers doffed their caps, and the party smiled and greeted them in return. There seemed to be no danger on this first leg of the journey, though there was some concern about the inn where they planned to stay that night, The Rose and Thorn. Inns were notorious places for thievery and even murder.

Before King Henry destroyed the monasteries, they had provided all travelers with safe places to rest and to dine, free of any charge for the poor. Travel in those days was not impossible for the poor as it was now, and the roads were mostly safe for everyone. But now there were only ruins where those havens had stood.

Inns had sprung up in the last several years to meet the needs of travelers that the monasteries had once met, but they were often more dangerous than the roads. The Rose and Thorn did not have a bad reputation, as many others had. Farther north, there was a Wingate property where they would have lodged had they been going so far in that direction. But tomorrow, before noon, they were to take a turn at a fork in the north road that would lead them toward Andersgate, to arrive sometime tomorrow evening.

What a joy to think of that arrival! Caroline allowed a smile to play a little on her lips, then settle there, where it seemed to be at home, happy to be there, as though it had been unwillingly absent for a long time.

Joseph turned his head and spoke over his shoulder. "My lady, will we stop to eat our dinner soon? It's long since breakfast, and we cannot get to the Rose afore supper."

"Yes, I think so, Joseph. Would you like to ride ahead and find a good place to stop and open the hamper?"

"Yes, ma'am. That's a fine idea. I'll ride back to tell you."

"Very good."

Joseph spurred his horse onward, leaving in the lead Norma, who disapproved of this impropriety and told Owen to move to the front. After a few moments, the horses and riders had rearranged themselves, all fell silent once more, and Caroline felt her spirits continuing to rise.

She was certain that John had not yet told her Aunt Margaret about Mary Posten; if he had, her aunt would surely have told her about it in her letters. It had been a few months now since John had written to tell her that he had met Mary on a trip to London and was quite taken with her. He had seen her again on subsequent trips, and he wanted to invite her to Andersgate but was afraid to mention it to his mother, afraid that she would have them married before they had had a chance to decide that for themselves. Caroline smiled. How wonderful it would be for Aunt Margaret to have John happily married, to have children again at Andersgate.

It was doubtful that Eleanor would ever marry. She knew Eleanor was a messenger for Catholic underground communication, and she traveled a great deal, though no one ever knew where she went. And it was no good asking Thompson, even though Caroline was sure he directed just about everything Eleanor did. She thought about how blessed the Anders family was in having Thompson with them, especially since her Uncle Ben had died ten years ago. Not only was he a figure of paternal strength for her cousins as they grew up, but he was as devoted to their faith as he was to the security and prosperity of Andersgate.

She felt guilty for feeling more affection for Thompson than for her own father. But then, affection for her father was not as important as obedience to him, not as important as filial loyalty, especially because he was so alone now since the death of her mother. It was obedience to her father that accounted for the unhappiness of her life now, and all thought of him brought the anguished mixture of love and sorrow, an anguish to which she had become so accustomed that it defined her life, not only today, but as far into the dark future as she dared to think.

She looked at Owen's back on the horse in front of her. He was small, Welsh, and a comely young man, full of good cheer and a wonder with the horses. Just then he asked over his shoulder, "My lady, would it please you to hear a bit of song to while away the time?"

"Oh, yes, Owen, that would be lovely."

"Well, I have my flute here in my kit," he patted his saddlebags, "but I can't play it and ride Ted here at the same time since he has to lead us, so I'll just sing a song for you, if you will. It's in my own tongue, ma'am. Afraid I don't know any English songs."

He launched into a very sprightly tune with a fast tempo, the kind of song it was easy to imagine dancing to. Caroline was surprised by his lovely voice and thought that the Welsh language added much to the lilting, dancing sound. When he finished with something of a flourish, she was delighted.

"Oh, wonderful, Owen! And you have a lovely voice. Tell me, what is the song about?"

"Oh, it's just one of the old tales about St. David, ma'am. But I've no voice. You should hear my sister Gwyneth—ah, now there's a voice."

"Owen, how does it happen that your family is in Devon?"

"Truth, ma'am?"

"Yes, of course."

"Well, it was in the Rebellion of '49, it was, my father Hugh was pressed into service to fight the rebels at Exeter, who wanted their church back—their real church, I mean. Well, his heart was not in it, ma'am, if you understand me. He was on their side. How was he to fight against his own fellows? Well, he just drifted off from camp one night, he said, and headed east, toward Blexton, dropping off the pike and bow in a lake as he went. And there he got work at Somerfield. Later on, when he thought it would be safe to do it—and with Sir Arnold's help—he sent for my mother and sister. Well, I was born there at Somerfield. I never have been to Wales, though it's my own tongue, from my mother and father at home, you know. And so, we are all there together now, at Somerfield." He paused. "I don't suppose you'd be wanting to inform on my father, ma'am? He's an old man now, you know."

"No, of course not. So you were at Somerfield when Sir Arnold lived in the house where we live now?"

"Yes, ma'am. He's a good man, Sir Arnold, a kind man. He knew all about my father, and he let us all stay, anyway."

"Yes, my husband and I have met him several times, and he is indeed a kind man. Thank you for telling me your story."

She lost herself then, her thoughts keeping the slow pace of the horses' hoofs, thudding softly on the path. Here was Owen's family, living in exile as servants in the house that her husband had leased from Sir Arnold, fearful still, perhaps, of returning home to their native Wales—yet holding to their Welsh language, music, and identity. There was exile everywhere. Silent sorrow. She thought of the lives of her own family, especially her father, living still in York as a stranger in his own beloved England. How many of us all, she thought, are exiles from our own hearts? How many are strangers in our own land? Thoughts of Owen's family made her overcome her own self-pity to wonder: *And how many of us are condemned to lives of infidelity and deceit?* She prayed silently for Owen's family, for her own, for people everywhere who now must live in shadow in their own country.

Her high spirits disappeared as that dark vision descended on her again, covering her in a chill, like a sudden cold fog. She could not bring herself out of it again, looking at Owen's small back in front of her, thinking of his family never free to feel safe, never able to attend Mass and take Holy Communion to give them strength for the life they must lead now, far from home and kin, for there was no priest at all in eastern Devonshire. She determined that when she returned to Somerfield, she would find some way to get them to their home, to Wales, but then she remembered that the persecution of Catholics in Wales and Ireland was even worse than it was in England. They were better off where they were now at Somerfield.

But what about Owen or Gwyneth if they wanted to marry, she wondered. Would they have to marry outside their Faith? Yes … her spirits sank lower than ever as she realized from her own unhappiness how true that answer was. Indeed, both Owen and Gwyneth were now past the age for young marriage — and now Caroline knew why they remained unmarried and childless. The family would die eventually, there at Somerfield.

Then, with an insight that was uncommon for her, since she avoided thinking about these matters, she realized the true nature and intent of the persecution that had been inflicted on faithful Catholics in England: It wasn't the violence of martyrdom that so afflicted them — that would have been easy. No. It was the slow, tortuously slow, bleeding — bleeding them until they died, until there was no life left in them, for the body cannot live without its soul. There was no death more calculated, more cruel, more final, than this slow bleeding.…

Joseph returned. "My lady, there is a right good clearing only three miles more."

* * *

In Devonshire that evening, Patricia Wilson was being mindful of her figure. She had enjoyed Betty's stew at dinner a little too much, a fact that normally would have caused her some regret, but tonight she and Andrew had been invited to dine with Sir Arnold, and it was better to go without a great appetite, for ladies, she knew, do not eat heartily in company. Andrew was brooding. That wasn't unusual, certainly, but he had questioned her rather too closely about her visit with Mrs. Braithlow, and it seemed that no answer, whether true or false, satisfied him. She had not returned in time to have dinner with him yesterday, and he had been busy in the evening with a burial, after which he had locked himself in his study. She had been able to avoid his questioning until this morning's breakfast.

"How did you find Mrs. Braithlow?"

"She was well enough."

"Patricia, I think you might be able to provide a few more particulars than 'well enough.'"

"Well, Andrew, what do you think? Do you think the woman should have welcomed me? The wife of a man whom she does not recognize as her pastor, paying an uninvited call? She's a traitor to her country and her faith!"

"She's no traitor to either, Patricia."

"So you say. Though the laws of England, the queen, and God himself say otherwise." She had felt her annoyance mounting and struggled to control herself.

"Patricia—"

"No, Andrew! You ordered me, *ordered* me to break the law."

"You are being ridiculous. There is no law that prohibits your paying a sick call on a parishioner, no matter who she is."

She grew shrill. "I will not do this again, Andrew. You cannot force me. The woman was rude—*rude*, I tell you. She did not invite me indoors but left me standing on her doorstep. She sent a servant to close the door in my face, Andrew. I might have fainted from humiliation right there, had not her son arrived."

Andrew tried to imagine Patricia in a faint of humiliation. "And what did he do to save you from such a fate?"

"Well, I must say he was very kind, very much a young gentleman—unlike the rest of his family. He came round the house just in time to catch me when I very nearly fell in faint."

"Ah," said Andrew, much amused at the imaginary scene of his wife falling into the strong young arms of one of the Braithlow boys. "Well, I am much comforted that you were rescued, my dear."

She did not mention to Andrew what she had heard during her visit to Mrs. Lewis, an ardent member of the queen's church. The woman had volunteered that she herself believed the Braithlows to be involved in activities far more treasonous than merely refusing to attend the English church. Her husband had lately overheard someone from the Braithlow farm talking at The Three Lions about how both of Josiah Braithlow's sons had arrived home in a great state of agitation two nights ago. Then lights were kindled in the kitchen and stayed on most of the night. And finally, before daybreak, Francis, the elder of the two, left the farm at great speed, heading away from the fields and the village, toward the northeast road, as though he were leaving Devonshire altogether.

Patricia had listened to this news with the closest attention; she was certain—and said so—that such strange goings-on appeared suspicious. But the last bit of information sealed her conviction that papist priests were being hidden on the farm: Mr. Braithlow had instructed his workman not to enter the barn that night! The workman was overheard to say that he didn't know what to make of it all.

Patricia did not mention any of this to Andrew; intuition told her to wait for an occasion when the information could be used to greater effect.

She called to Betty below stairs to come and lace her sleeves, thinking again that she needed a personal maid. She was wearing her blue woolen dress with the white lace collar. There was no embroidery or ornamentation at all on the dress, but at least it was fine wool, not the coarse kind that peasants wore.

Andrew would be in his tiresome gray, of course, his clothes indistinguishable from his own grayness. She sighed heavily. No one would ever know how difficult it was to be married to a parson, who did nothing but read—and a man twice her age, at that. She could not know, looking at the mirror with both approval and despair, that her husband was below stairs enjoying very much the prospect of seeing her discover that Sir Arnold's supper party included Captain Wingate—more than that, Captain Wingate without his wife, who had left on a visit to her kin in Somerset. The supper was intended to celebrate the captain's appointment as magistrate.

* * *

Sir Arnold Somers and his wife, Maryanne, were quite elderly. He had actually been the son of a yeoman, but like his father, he worked hard, purchased still more land than his father had done, and finally attained a peerage. He was landlord to the rectory, to Somerfield, to most of the land in that area of Devonshire. It was the great personal tragedy of the Somerses that they had no heir to inherit the fruit of Sir Arnold's hard work and thrift. As it was, his wastrel nephew in Plymouth would inherit everything. Perhaps for that reason, they were exceptionally fond of young Captain Wingate and his beautiful and well-mannered wife.

Their fondness was certainly no condescension on their part: Edward would inherit a title someday, and the Wingate holdings were far greater than their own, despite the fact that the young heir had been almost penniless until his marriage to Caroline, the daughter of a very wealthy merchant in the north. They knew that the Wingates' tenure in Devon would be brief; Edward would assume control of the Wingate estate in a few short years and perhaps even resign his commission, but, by some unspoken agreement between them, they had treated the Wingates as their own children, rather than as their tenants, and would continue for as long as they might.

Edward was enjoying the evening, though he missed Caroline. He regretted his decision now to permit her to visit her family. But that regret was not as painful as the happiness he had seen in her eyes when he gave his permission—made so much worse by her instinctive attempt to conceal it. Sir Arnold had planned quite a feast in his honor: grouse, lamb, lovely puddings—and some really splendid wines from France. He was surprised to see that the wine steward was an old man, not the young man he had seen in The Three Lions, but he smiled as he remembered what Maude had said: Potty Deeters spoke more than he knew. Who the young man was, talking with Josiah Braithlow at the tavern, would now remain a mystery.

Reverend Wilson and his strange wife, Patricia, were there. He still chafed at the near-rebuke he had received from the reverend yesterday, but he had to admit that perhaps it was deserved. Mrs. Wilson was not a congenial table companion; her piercing black eyes always looked as though she wanted to devour him. She made inane remarks and laughed at her own witless humor, never taking her eyes off him. He felt embarrassed for the reverend.

One of the servants at Somerfield had told him that Andrew Wilson had once been a Catholic priest when he was a very young man, until the queen determined that there would be no more Catholic priests in England. Celibacy was not required of clergy in the English church, and several years ago, he had married Patricia, a peasant's pretty daughter from Blakely Down who wanted to escape her fate as a peasant's wife. He suspected that the decision had been unwise, that the reverend might regret it now.

Two men from London were also among the party, guests of the Somers, who were introduced simply as Mr. White and Mr. Bentwood. As members of their class, the Somerses were obligated to entertain any visitors from Court. The gentlemen had just arrived that afternoon. They said they were on their way to the port in Plymouth on business for Her Majesty. Though they seemed very pleasant—even charming—Edward knew they were actually Lord Walsingham's spies. The whole country was infested with them since the militia had been raised to pursue hidden Catholic priests. He wondered briefly if they knew about the killings at the Leacham farm somehow—but the reports that he and Robert had written to the Commission had not had time to reach London yet, so he didn't think they could know anything about it. And unless he was asked, he would not volunteer any information.

Robert Marley and his wife, Louise, were also in attendance, mitigating the pressure he felt to be always entertained by Patricia Wilson. Supper had been superb, and the party had now retired to the drawing room to be entertained by Sir Arnold's harpist. Then Robert, standing behind his wife's chair with his hand on her shoulder, leaned forward to speak to the reverend: "It was very good of you to do what you did yesterday, sir."

Andrew raised his brows and lazily waved his fingers in the air. "Not at all, Sheriff Marley. You did well to call on me."

Robert appeared mollified, as though his rebuke had been lifted.

Patricia asked, "And what would that good deed be, Sheriff Marley?"

Robert answered, "Your husband, ma'am, presided at the burial of three outlaws yesterday evening."

"Oh?" Patricia's eyes pierced Robert's. "What sort of outlaws?"

"Some papist spies, ma'am. Three of them," said Robert, wishing suddenly that he had not mentioned it.

"Oh, my. And my husband would have them buried in the churchyard, I'm sure." She spoke with a measure of bitterness that surprised the others. "But tell me, how did you come upon the traitors? Where did you find them?"

Robert felt a reluctance to speak further, though he wasn't sure why, but since he himself had brought the subject up, there was nothing for it. "Well, ma'am, a farmer came upon them in his barn, having some kind of meeting, and shot them."

"Good heavens! How awful," Lady Somers remarked. "Why on earth did he shoot them? I hope you've arrested him. Those poor people. But why were they in his barn, I wonder."

"It seems the meeting had been arranged by one of his workers, who thought the farmer would be away from home," answered Robert.

"And was the farmer's name Braithlow?" Patricia fairly spurted the question, which sounded more like a demand than a question.

"No," answered Robert, who wondered why the Braithlows should even be suggested, since they were known recusants and would scarcely be suspected of killing papists. "It was Farmer Leacham who shot them."

"Patricia! I do think the sheriff's business is best left to the sheriff." Andrew spoke firmly.

"Well, Andrew, I ask only because I know that Mr. Braithlow allows *no one* to enter his barn! Not even his workers." There. She'd said it at just the right time. Everyone sat up straight in their chairs, and Lady Somers paled a bit. Louise shifted her weight in her chair and took Robert's hand where it had been resting on her shoulder. But, best of all, Andrew's mouth opened—and then closed without a word, though his eyes held obvious anger. And the two gentlemen from London cast furtive looks at each other and leaned forward in their chairs. Sir Arnold told the harpist to play another melody.

* * *

Father Clive Farwell sat down at his desk in Bath. He rubbed the tops of his thighs and his kneecaps with crippled fingers; his legs, sensitive to cold, were aching, and he knew he should start a fire. His housekeeper, Mrs. MacDonald, had offered to start a fire for him, but he wanted to conserve fuel whenever he could. He expected the arrival of the new priest from Devon sometime tomorrow, when young Braithlow would have had time to return to Devon with the only good riding horse the family had. And he would have to give him the disappointing news that he could not be sent to any location near his family, as he knew the priest expected. Since the arrest of Father Joseph, the new priest would have to go west to the hill country, where the Anders lived, for there was now no priest at all west of Bath. He wished he could at least allow the new priest a visit to his family, but that would not be possible for some little while now.

He rubbed his tired eyes with his gnarled fingers. Giving the priest that sad news was not as dreadful as the task that confronted him now. He had spent the last half hour in prayer, then took up his pen, knowing exactly how he should proceed. It was always that way: he prayed for one grace and received quite another. He had prayed for strength; what he received was simple clarity—and he found in that clarity that it was not strength he had needed. He knew what to say in the letter he must write to the Anders and Johnson families. The letter would be delivered by the new priest, though it would be a sad introduction for him.

He decided that he would have a fire now, after all, and then write the letter. He called to Mrs. MacDonald to have her son Sam come and light the fire, rubbed his fingers to warm them, and pressed the collar of his heavy woolen dressing gown against the back of his neck. As a retired schoolmaster, he was afflicted by poverty, often severely, but he had several very kind neighbors who provided for him out of their own means, even though they were Protestants and knew very well that he was a Catholic priest. He often thanked God for them, not only because they were helpful to him, but also because they kept him in constant awareness that no one, not even the queen, could set limits on God's mercy. And it was good to be reminded that the evil of England's queen had not tainted every English soul.

The evil of England's queen had steeped her soul in damnation long past any point at which the pope might declare her excommunicated, so that when he finally did so, the action was laughably superfluous, like a macabre joke, met with ridicule in England. But there had finally been limits for the Holy Father—though they were far beyond the theft of all the Church's property, beyond the slaughter of his holy priests, limits that were finally met only by the murder of innocent children.

Only God had no limits to his patience, his love and mercy. There was no price he would not pay for the salvation of his children. He had not spared his own chosen people, had not spared his only-begotten Son; should his Church expect to be spared? Should her children even desire it? The reading for Mass that very day had been from St. Paul's letter to the Romans:

> What will separate us from the love of Christ? Will anguish, or distress, or persecution, or famine, or nakedness, or peril, or the sword? As it is written: "For your sake we are slain all the day long; we are looked upon as sheep to be slaughtered." No, in all these things, we conquer overwhelmingly through him who loved us. For I am convinced that neither death, nor life, nor angels, nor principalities, nor present things, nor future things, nor powers, nor height, nor depth, nor any other creature will be able to separate us from the love of God in Christ Jesus our Lord.

He dipped his quill now in the precious ink, so expensive, knowing that he had needed no strength; his very weakness was his strength.

"My dear children in Christ …" he began.

*　*　*

It was dusk when Caroline arrived at The Rose and Thorn. It was well lit, she was relieved to see, and there appeared to be many travelers inside. She sent Owen in to see the innkeeper about rooms and supper while she and Norma waited outside, still on horseback. Joseph stayed with them. Norma was surprised to see so much business at the inn and worried that rooms might not be available for them. She dismounted and handed her reins to Joseph, announcing that she would *demand* space. Fortunately, however, Owen returned and told the party that there were rooms enough for sleeping, but all the dining tables were in use. They would have to share a table. In fear that his mistress might refuse, Joseph let out a low moan, but Caroline said that sharing a table would be quite acceptable, and the ostler took her reins while his helper took Norma's. Joseph was already near the door when Owen said that he would tend to the horses and eat later.

The innkeeper met them at the doorway, bowed low to Caroline, and pointed toward the kitchen when he saw Joseph, but Norma said, "My lady, I think Joseph should stay with us, at least until Owen returns." Caroline nodded. Leading the three of them, the innkeeper approached a young man sitting at a table alone, his back turned toward Caroline and her party. He leaned over the young man's shoulder to speak quietly into his ear. Instantly, the young man sprang up, turned, and bowed in Caroline's direction without raising his eyes. She nodded slightly and approached the other end of the table, followed by Norma, who maintained a very cautious survey of both the room and the young man. He did not resume his seat until Caroline was seated; then he nodded toward her and smiled. "Good evening, my lady," he said.

She raised her eyes to Stephen's and smiled. He could not afterward remember that smile, or even her face, as well as he wished. He remembered instead the rustle of her silk riding skirts, the scent of roses as she peeled off her yellow leather gloves, and the astonishing whiteness of her small hands. He remembered also the small narrow shoulders, bowed slightly in their fatigue, in puffed green velvet sleeves on either side of a gold-embroidered bodice, and a charming little riding cap with a yellow feather, over bound curls the color of toasted walnuts on a Christmas pudding. That was what he remembered in the months that followed. He could never remember her eyes.

As for Caroline, she could remember only Stephen's eyes, gray, calm, and deep, like the sea. "Good evening, sir," she replied.

* * *

Later, as she lay in the feather-stuffed bed upstairs, surprisingly large and comfortable, Caroline thought about how odd it was that the presence of the rather small young man at the end of their table should so fill the room—full as it was of many other diners. She attributed the sensation to the fact that she had never shared a table with a stranger before. Down the hall, Stephen lay awake on a pallet amid the snores of men sleeping together in the large dormitory-style bedroom. He was resisting sleep, clinging to a pleasing sound of rustling green silk, a vision of a yellow feather that moved gently with an endearing absurdity. Finally, he fell asleep, enveloped by the fragrance of sunlit English roses.

5

Norma rose early, dressed in the darkness, and went below stairs to make arrangements for her mistress. She was gratified to find that the kitchen was already astir. She got the warm water she sought for the pitcher she had carried with her, and a mug of mead, some fresh bread and cheese, and headed back up the stairs with the heavy tray. On the way, she met the young man with whom they had shared a table last evening. He offered to help her and asked if they had had a comfortable night. She declined his offer and said yes, their night had been tolerable, without thanking him for his inquiry, thinking that there was no reason her lady Caroline's comfort should concern him.

Detecting her ill-concealed disdain, Stephen replied, "My regards to your mistress, ma'am."

Norma was offended by what she took to be his effrontery. "Sir, I have doubt that my mistress should have need of your regard."

He only nodded and continued his descent down the stairs, leaving Norma feeling more than a little ashamed of her remark. After all, at supper last night, he had been very courteous. He had made no forward attempt to engage them in conversation, and when he departed from their shared table, he bowed to Caroline and repeated again, "Good evening, my lady." Caroline had nodded to him in return for his courtesy. There was no cause for Norma to be rude to him now.

Outside in the yard, Stephen waited for the stableman to saddle Stella. He didn't know how she would be returned to Devonshire, but he knew that until she was returned, the Braithlows would have no horse if they should need one. He thought about seeing his parents and his two younger brothers soon and smiled with quiet joy—how happy he would be to see them all. It had been six long years. He took the reins and was pleased to see that Stella had apparently been well tended and fed. She nudged him on his chest, tamping her forelegs softly, ready to go. He mounted and looked heavenward: the morning sky after last night's slow, gentle rain was washed clean, a great canopy of glistening blue satin, freshly unfurled. A soft breeze caressed his face, warm and comforting, and it rustled the leaves of the overhanging elm trees, causing their raindrops to sprinkle down lightly on his head and tunic. He felt newly baptized, blessed, almost anointed somehow.

He thought of the young woman who had shared his table last night. He felt certain that he knew her somehow, though he could not remember where or when he had known her. From time to time, he had glanced in her direction—not often, because her protective servant caught his eye every time with a stern glare of her own—and each time, he was more convinced that everything about her was familiar: the movement of her wrist when she cut her meat, the way she tilted her head to listen to her servant's speech. Even the sharing of a table seemed somehow familiar, like something forgotten and suddenly remembered. He could not say that her voice was familiar, since she spoke very little, and when she did, her voice was too low to hear. He had no trouble hearing her servant's voice, however, and judging from what he heard, they were traveling to visit some of the lady's kin. He wished he could have had some little conversation with her, to find out who she was and where he had known her. He thought she was the most beautiful woman he had ever seen.

Stella started a slow trot out of the yard as his hand slipped down to his kit to find his rosary. He would reach Father Farwell's house in Bath before nightfall, earlier, perhaps, than he was expected. Francis Braithlow had given him careful directions to the house in Compton Lane; he felt sure he'd find it with no difficulty. At the fork in the road a few miles straight ahead, he was to take the northeast road toward Bath. There was, so Francis had said, a ruin there of a small convent, St. Anne's. Perhaps because of its small size, it had somehow escaped King Henry's destruction of the monasteries, but it was destroyed later by his son, the boy king Edward. Since Stephen was ahead of his schedule, he would stop a while. Meanwhile, on this beautiful morning, under rustling elm leaves, beneath a blue satin sky, he was sublimely content to be on Stella's back, his rosary in his hand, and unaccountably happy for the first time since he arrived in Devon. It was a happiness that, at least for the moment, was unclouded by the self-questioning that haunted him so often.

Upstairs in the inn, Norma was folding Caroline's linen and placing it in the small woven hamper for Joseph to take below stairs to the packhorse. She had slept very well on the cot next to her mistress's bed, happy that the sheets were clean and free of lice, and she was happy now to see that the bit of kindling had made such a nice little fire for her mistress. Caroline was putting her arms into her bodice now and paused. "Norma, go find Joseph, please, and give him this purse to give the innkeeper. Tell him to express gratitude that we have had such a comfortable night and such good food. Then he is to come and take the packs below stairs to the horses."

"Yes, my lady. But you'll be wanting more to eat for breakfast than that bit of bread and cheese, won't you, ma'am?"

"No, I don't think so. We have some apples. I think I will just have one of those if I get hungry later, and there is enough salted

pork, cheese, and bread for our dinner. We should reach Andersgate before nightfall if this lovely weather holds, but perhaps not
if we take a long breakfast. And if you don't find Owen in the
kitchen, look for him in the stables, where he will likely be making certain the horses have been tended."

"Yes, ma'am." Norma left the room, and Caroline took her
prayer book from her bag and sat down on the bed to say her
morning prayers. She had made the Sign of the Cross to begin
when she was arrested by the memory of the young man who
had shared their table the night before. When he stood to bow,
she saw that he was only a little taller than she was, and his
frame was slight. Whatever his trade, he was clearly not a workman. Yet his dress was simple—a brown woolen tunic—but
when she caught a fleeting glimpse of him as they ate their supper, she saw that his eyes were kind and gentle, and full of intel-
ligence. Perhaps he was a student. It was his eyes that aroused
her curiosity; he seemed oddly familiar. She might have enjoyed
a little conversation to discover more about him but for Norma's
protectiveness. She felt embarrassed by Norma's rudeness but
then a little guilty to be embarrassed: she knew very well that
her servant only wanted to protect her.

Norma found Joseph in the kitchen, where he was deeply
involved with a good deal of bacon. Owen was nowhere in sight.
"Where is Owen?" she asked Joseph.

Between large mouthfuls of black bread and bacon, he mo-
tioned with his knife, "Stable."

As Caroline's personal servant, Norma had visited her lady's
aunt once before and was a little proud of her knowledge. "Now,
Joseph, you'll be in the lead again, and you must remember
when we come to the fork in the road, you're to take the north-
west road, for that's the way to Andersgate." Then she spoke to
the cook as she left through the back door of the kitchen, "If
you have some bread and a little butter, I would be thankful."

She thought about it only briefly before deciding that it would be best if she herself gave the purse to the innkeeper, rather than Joseph. Outside, Owen was indeed in the stable, saddling the horses. Norma saw the blanket rolled up in the corner on the straw and knew that Owen had slept there, inside the stall with the horses. "Owen, you should come and eat some breakfast now, for we must leave soon." Without answering, he put aside the bridle he held and followed her to the kitchen.

Upstairs, Caroline concluded her Morning Office. Apart from her usual prayer, she felt an impulse to pray for her father. Though the bond between them had been close since the death of her mother, there was also a barrier now, since her forced marriage, a barrier that she could do nothing about, for, as much as she loved her father, she had a greater love, and she had begged her father to allow her to enter the convent in France. He couldn't bear the thought of losing her, however, not even to Christ. He was a faithful Catholic, if not a devout one, and he knew he should not restrain her; moreover, he knew that no Catholic was safe in England—though his love for England was second only to his love for her. He tried to believe that her passion was only the natural longings of a virgin ready for marriage. In the end, he compensated for his unacknowledged selfishness by an insistence that she make a "safe" marriage to someone who would be above any suspicion of disloyalty to the Crown, someone who was utterly "un-Catholic," as he put it, though not a zealous reformer—preferably someone more or less indifferent to religion. He'd met Sir Thomas Wingate on a business trip to London and knew of his financial problems and his constant pursuit of connections at Court. He knew also that Sir Thomas had an unmarried son, heir to the Wingate lands, who was in the queen's navy, a patriotic and socially respectable profession.

Caroline's heart was broken when the marriage was arranged, and she never recovered. Instead, despite her resolve, which she tried to renew daily, it seemed that she descended ever deeper into a sense of desolation. She had understood all her father's reasoning in the matter, knowing that he had done the best he could have done. Since the death of her mother, her father's two great loves were England and his daughter. He could not leave the one, nor could he bear to let the other go. And so the "safe" Protestant marriage was arranged. Caroline often prayed now that her father would never understand what his love had cost her, that he would die without ever knowing. No one knew except her Aunt Margaret.

She closed her prayer book and then her eyes. There was some little time for meditation before she went below stairs. She breathed her morning greeting, "*Gloria Patri et Filio*—" but stopped, suddenly interrupted by the vision of a simple color: a deep gray, full of peace, moving slowly and gently, like waves on a calm sea.

* * *

In Devonshire that morning, Edward sat in a chair before a cold hearth in his library. His hands extended under the sleeves of his black brocaded dressing gown over the arms of the chair. In his right hand he held a letter from his mother between his fingertips. His life, he mused, was controlled by the post. A letter from the Lord Admiral had announced his commission, a letter from his father had informed him of his betrothal to Caroline, and only two days ago, a letter on behalf of the queen had made him a magistrate. And now another letter, this one from Lady Lydia Wingate, would change his life completely.

His father was gravely ill. His mother felt that he should come at once. He thought about how ashen his father's face had looked when he saw him last, and he knew the end had come. So many thoughts crowded his mind that he found it hard to sort them out, to focus on one at a time in order to assimilate this news and all that it meant for his life, his future—and what it should mean to him personally.

He noticed first the absence of any feeling. He had never been close to his father, never felt they had much in common. He had been sent away to school earlier than most boys and visited home less often. When he did return home, his father was never there. He was always away somewhere, often at Court in London, trying to make some kind of profitable connection, sometimes just out hunting or gaming. But his mother was always there, always happy to see him, and his bond with her had always been strong. After school, he had been apprenticed to Captain Ludlow in the navy, and he had returned home rarely since then, though he'd kept a correspondence with his mother. Sometimes he thought of Caroline's relationship with her own family, with her father in York, and he wondered whether he should feel deprived. He didn't know, but the fact was that he did not. How could he feel a loss of something he had never had? It wasn't possible—and that thought brought Caroline herself to his mind, though he didn't see the connection, and he let it go.

He traced his lips with his left forefinger, then down his clean-shaven chin and throat, looking up at the ceiling. He would take possession of all the Wingate lands, leave Devonshire, where he had never been happy. *This is what I have always really wanted; this is what I have been waiting for. Why have I not thought of it before, not consciously desired it? Because it would be reprehensible to desire the death of my father? Yes, of course.* He felt surprised by this discovery—self-examination had never been a preoccupation for him. His abhorrence of moral guilt had created a personality that received fortune, rather than created it. Now he was realizing that he felt relief, as though an obstacle had been removed *for* him, unexpected, undesired, a boon not sought *by* him. He smiled, feeling a sense of self-approval. He saw himself now, with Caroline's significant dowry, taking control of Wingate Hall and all its lands. He would build a new house. His thoughts were suddenly racing with plans—improvements to the estates. For, unlike his father, Sir Edward Wingate would have more than land—he would have wealth. It occurred to him then that he had not placed Caroline in that image of his future, and he had a strange, fleeting foreboding that he would never see his wife again.

She had been such a surprise; he had not expected William Nelson's daughter to be the delight she was. In fact, he had taken the side of his mother in arguing against the marriage arrangement: a match with a merchant's daughter was below a man of his station. Though bad investments by his grandfather, and then also by his father, had left the Wingates with very little wealth, they still held considerable land. His mother's hopes for her husband's advancement at Court had died long ago, but she still harbored a hope for her only child, Edward. Marriage into the merchant class would not advance that desire, but the Nelson wealth would be an advantage.

Privately, after his father had told him about Caroline's impressive dowry, he had added, "Besides—consider, my son, the gratitude a low-born woman would bring to your marriage bed." Well, Edward thought with some bitterness, there had been none of that. His father had been wrong about that, just as he had been wrong about his investments. It was the first time Edward had ever felt any sort of dissatisfaction at all where Caroline was concerned, and the realization surprised him. Why? He looked at the letter again, at his mother's handwriting. Because, he thought, because *this* is what is mine, my own. Caroline has never been mine....

The thought shocked him. He felt as though he had accidentally opened a door he hadn't meant to open, one he might wish he had left undisturbed.

His thoughts were interrupted by Alice, who entered to say that a Mr. White and a Mr. Bentwood were calling on him. After Patricia Wilson's outburst the night before, he knew what the visit would be about — the Braithlows. He had had some hope that her remark had gone unnoticed, but not much; he had seen the reaction of the two "gentlemen from London." Dread filled him: They were wasting no time. Yes, he would indeed resign as magistrate very soon now — the office put him in such an awkward position. Aloud, he said, "Have them wait in the hall a moment."

He folded the letter and put it aside on the table next to his chair. Surely, they merely wanted to consult him for his judgment on the loyalty of the Braithlows, and of course, he would assure them of it, though he had no idea about it. He had never actually met the farmer and knew nothing about the family, but he would claim some hearsay knowledge to prevent harm to Braithlow. He felt certain that would satisfy them, and the unpleasant incident could be forgotten. He rose and went to the hall to greet his guests.

"Good morning, gentlemen. It's a pleasure to see you again. What business brings you here?"

Bentwood extended his hand and spoke first. "Sorry to trouble you so soon after our acquaintance last evening, Captain, but there is a matter we need to discuss briefly with you."

Edward led them into the drawing room and offered them chairs, noticing that Bentwood closed the door behind them and dropped his voice.

"Thank you, sir," he said, drawing his chair closer to Edward's. He went directly to his purpose: "As you may have surmised, Captain, we are in the employ of Lord Walsingham at Whitehall. Do you know who that gentleman is?" Edward nodded. "Then you may also know that Her Majesty has despaired of patient persuasion with the treasonous recalcitrance of papist elements in our country, with their schemes against the throne of Her Majesty, and their conspiracies to surrender England into the hands of the Romish pope to be looted and plundered by his puppet Spain."

Edward cleared his throat and made a conscious effort to keep his face at once serious and attentive by frowning, inclining his head slightly, and placing his forefinger against his temple while his thumb supported his chin, resting his elbow on the arm of his chair. He hoped he looked as though he took such nonsense seriously, that he was giving the impression of a thoughtful reflection on Bentwood's words. He could feel Mr. White watching him closely. He waited to be asked for his opinion of Josiah Braithlow.

"How may I assist you, sirs?"

It appeared to be exactly the response the two men sought. Both of them made slight settling movements in their chairs. White cleared his throat then and spoke for the first time. He explained their plan to surround the Braithlow farm with specially chosen "persons"—he did not use the word *militia*—to see if the Braithlows were harboring strangers there.

Edward was caught off guard; they weren't seeking his judgment in the matter at all. For a moment, he felt helpless and confused. Then, to counteract the feeling, he decided it was a relief to know that action against the Braithlows would not be immediate or direct—and he was even more relieved to know that he would not be expected to participate in any action. Their intention "to keep a watchful eye" was innocent enough and required nothing of him. Surely, someone had already alerted the Braithlow family—Sir Arnold, perhaps, or Reverend Wilson—and they would exercise sensible care, if indeed any strangers were staying there—which he had no reason to believe.

Mr. White said, "We merely wanted to alert you, sir, that there is an unfortunate possibility that your service as magistrate may be required. And of course, we would not have spoken so frankly with you had we not complete trust in your discretion."

"Of course," Edward responded. The two men rose to leave. He led them to the door with the assurance of both his assistance and his discretion. They had not asked for his judgment; they wanted no opinion of his on the subject of Josiah Braithlow, and he wondered for a moment what they did want, why they had troubled to inform him of their plans. To "alert" him seemed a superfluous motive. No. Their purpose had been to *instruct* him—to inform him of their *expectation* of him. That awareness was followed immediately by an understanding of his hasty appointment as magistrate. The Crown wanted swift favorable judgment of Walsingham's actions in Devonshire, and Edward had been perceived as one who would provide it. That was all.

It was as though, when he realized that Caroline was not his own, he had opened a door that now allowed other knowledge—equally painful and unwelcome—to enter. He knew with certainty then that his position was not to wield authority at all, but to submit to it; not to decide anything, but to give legitimacy to others' decisions. In the suddenness of that insight, he saw more than he wanted to see. It was *all* of a piece, he thought—like his position under Captain Ludlow, in the absurd raids on the Spanish coast, to provoke reaction from Spain, to make Spain become a threat to England in order to legitimize the queen's hatred.

And now this: Even the English were a threat to her—if they were Catholic—even the harmless Farmer Braithlow must be seen as a threat, a traitor, to England. The lengths, which should have been unthinkable, that the queen would go to in order to protect *herself*—certainly not England. And now he was caught up in it, in Walsingham's net of spies, persecuting harmless religious citizens in his own country.

He had never been able to shake the memory of a child, a small boy who looked to be about seven or eight years old, running frantically, desperately, along the harbor in Cadiz, trying to escape the English guns. When the smoke cleared, he could see the child lying face down in blood. And still the Spanish King Philip had not responded—though this raid was not the first, nor would it be the last.

What made that child running along the harbor England's enemy? Was the child England's enemy? And was he the enemy because he was Spanish—or was it simply because he was a Catholic—and therefore, his very existence seen as a threat. How many more would have to die to make the queen feel secure—and not just the people of Spain now, but her own people? And the English themselves—they cooperated now in this persecution of their own people by their intense nationalism, turning their country and their monarch into a single object of worshipful passion.

Edward sank back down into his chair in the library, the letter on the table forgotten for the moment. He felt intense disgust. The image of Beryl at The Three Lions, in that foul-smelling room, sprang unaccountably to his mind—why, he didn't know—except that it seemed to be symbolic of all that was happening to his countrymen, especially those with political ambitions. And he—against his own will—had been made a part of it, woven into the fabric of it all with no way out. He felt a chill remembering Elizabeth's small eyes, eyes that read his revulsion as quickly and as thoughtlessly as a blackbird seizes a worm in its beak.

In a moment, without any further thought or reflection on its causes, Edward picked up the letter from his mother and realized the narrowness of his true affection. It wasn't so much a change as it was a sudden awareness of what already was: all that mattered to him was in his hand at this moment. It was all that was his own. Everything else he regarded with contempt, indifference, or both—his commission, his country. And now, stripped of his ever-present desire for her by the sudden shock of his self-awareness, his disregard included even the stranger who was his wife.

He would have to wait until Caroline returned from Somerset, and then he would leave Devonshire and resign his position as magistrate and his commission in the navy. He would begin preparations now—immediately—even before Caroline returned, and as soon as possible, he would go *home*. He would keep his distance from Court as best he could. All he wanted was to mind his estates and try to live in safety and privacy. If he avoided all politics, all public involvement, he might be able to forget the child in Cadiz, for above all else, he would keep his own conscience clear. But for now, for today, he would have to settle just to be relieved that he would have no part to play in the horror that he feared would soon descend on the Braithlow farm.

* * *

At the rectory, breakfast had not gone too badly for Patricia. Andrew's customary silence was more profound, even condemning, but her triumph of last evening was still pleasantly warm in her memory. Not only had she succeeded in surprising Andrew with her knowledge of village affairs, but it was obvious she had impressed all the other guests as well—especially the two gentlemen from London. She felt quite pleased with herself and thought that Andrew might now take more seriously her opinions on the proper response to recusants. She was in her room dressing in her best gown, the elegant black damask, having decided to visit Mrs. Lewis and share the news of her triumph. After all, it was very impressive to have such connections as the gentlemen from London. A visit to Mrs. Lewis would affirm the feeling of righteous importance she now enjoyed. It would also ensure that the entire parish would know of her worth.

Andrew had retired to his study, as was his custom. He knew who the two men were at Sir Arnold's home last night. Everyone knew, everyone except Patricia. He reflected on his wife's wordless gloating at breakfast. There was an enviable innocence in her ignorance. He felt very old looking down at his hands, the flaccid skin covering gnarled knuckles, blue veins prominent, in rehearsal for decay. He would die soon. A peaceful death of old age. Not the death that possibly awaited Josiah Braithlow now, the death of a martyr.... He should go now, he knew, at this very moment, to the Braithlow farm and warn them, but even as the thought occurred to him, he knew he would not go. He would do as he had always done: either stand aside or get in line, whatever was required of him. And so he went instead to the cupboard that held his volume of Latin commentary on Irenaeus and prepared to sit by his window and resume his reading. At that moment, a cloud passed over the bright morning sun outside, and his prie-dieu stood in the corner in shadow, like an empty gallows waiting for him. Unable now to avoid looking at it, his true motive for the life he had chosen stood out in stark relief against that shadow.

Meanwhile, at the Marley home, Louise and Robert lingered over breakfast. Louise had just asked her husband if there would be trouble for the Braithlows, but before Robert could reply, he saw through his window two gentlemen riding up to his front door. He knew that her question would be answered by that arrival.

* * *

In Somerset, the clatter of cutlery and plate at the Anders breakfast table seemed horribly loud to Margaret. Louder still were the remarks of John and Thompson, addressed to each other, almost as if she were not there — remarks about the estates, about the amount of cheese the dairy would produce, about problems John was having with an agent at Dover or someplace. Margaret could hardly follow the conversation. The loudest thing was the silence, a silence that could not be covered by cutlery or conversation. It seemed to Margaret that the more noise her table companions made, the louder the silence became. They heard it too, and finally it became unbearable. John announced he must go to Dover and deal with the problem there. Responding to his mother's look of disbelieving shock, he hastened to add that he wouldn't be leaving for a few days yet. For now, he'd go upstairs and write the agent, have Richard arrange a courier, and so on. No, he wasn't planning to leave for several days yet. Then Thompson's chair scraped backward — he had to visit one of the farms, he said. Margaret knew he was going to the Johnson farm. She knew he was thinking of the fear the Johnsons were feeling, worrying about their son Charles, about why he had not returned from his trip escorting Eleanor. What would he say to them? What had he *not* said to *her*?

John kissed her forehead and left to go upstairs to Richard. She was left at the table alone, staring down at the pieces of bread she had torn from the loaf and left untouched, pieces of her heart, broken, left unspoken to, in silence. She was angry. Did they think she was a fool? Did they think that if they didn't say anything about Eleanor, about the delay in her return — too loud now not to hear — the silence would just make the fear go away?

* * *

On the road to Bath, fields of young wheat, oats, and barley, bordered by low hedgerows and interrupted here and there by small stretches of wood, lay still and peaceful by the road. Stephen had encountered no fellow travelers on the road so far, had seen no workmen in the fields. The growing season had begun now; there was not so much for workmen to do, as the fields themselves took over the work of growing. Gold and green under a warm sun, how blessed it all seemed to Stephen, how glorious in its quiet growth, its slow and silent fulfillment.

Around midday, he reached the fork in the road. Taking the road to the right would bring him to Bath well before dusk. But in the middle of the fork was an overgrown path, almost invisible in the tangle of wood and undergrowth. Francis had told him that the path led to the ruin of St. Anne's convent, about half a mile ahead. On the other side of the convent, the path continued at a sharp right turn to join the road to Bath. The low-hanging limbs of the trees looked a little threatening, so he dismounted and led Stella behind him as he walked the path amid the stillness that only a forest, untended and wild, can possess.

He passed a few tumbled stones and thought he would approach a clearing before the ruin came into view, but instead it appeared suddenly, all at once among the trees. It was very small. The primary means of destruction of the monasteries had been the simple removal of their roofs. The weather worked quickly once the roof was removed. But apparently St. Anne's had been made of wood and burnt; only the gray foundation stones remained.

There was no sign of any broken statuary or any other sort of artwork the convent might have possessed. It was doubtful there had been much to destroy in such a small sanctuary, but whatever there was, it would have been the first thing put to the torch, along with any Bibles or other manuscripts. Such things had been declared "pagan." How ironic, Stephen thought, since it was the monasteries that had civilized pagan Britain, a land whose people were nothing more than warring tribes, offering up human sacrifices to deified nature spirits. Except for the Gospel itself, the greatest gift of the monasteries had been civilization. But, he thought, there is something in man that hungers for the exaltation of his own will, that thirsts after his own glory, something that longs for violence, for conquest and power—something that refuses to be civilized.

The destruction of the monasteries had happened two generations before Stephen was born, and tragic as it was, it was never personally meaningful for him. For him, it simply meant that he had to leave his country in order to enter a seminary, and that he had to return as a priest in secret, risking lives—other lives as well as his own. It was never properties, or even history, that Stephen thought about; it was always people who occupied his thoughts. For him, the destruction of the monasteries meant the priests, monks, and nuns who were forced out of them, the many craftsmen and farmers—laypersons—who had lived and farmed on monastery lands for generations beyond count, whole families suddenly made homeless with no alternative to starvation but to become beggars. Worse still was what it meant for the elderly and the disabled, for whom the monasteries had been havens. In fact, in the wake of the dissolution of the monasteries, the number of vagrants grew so great that vagrancy was made a crime, and imprisonment became the punishment for destitution.

Wandering now among the gray stones, he saw only the suffering and destruction of the people. Faces rose before his eyes—faces of those he had never known rose and faded, became the faces of the Braithlows, of his parents and brothers, of his classmates at Oxford, of the priest there, saying Mass in the light of one dim candle in a cellar … faces.

He located the place where the path continued, heading due east back to the road to Bath, then mounted his horse and sat looking back at the small outline of stones. He thought he should feel sorrow for such destruction, and he did feel the immensity of the tragedy, the irrevocable loss. But the faces remain, he thought, both those he knew and many thousands of others he would never see. While they remained, he could not mourn too deeply for churches or monasteries. And while they remained, so would he.

* * *

Caroline had waited until they were well on their way on the north road to tell Norma that she should instruct Joseph to stop before taking the turn westward at the fork, into Somerset. She had never been able to stop at the ruin of St. Anne's before. On her two visits to Somerset since her marriage, Edward had been with her. This was her first trip alone. When they arrived at the pathway, the party had mixed reactions.

Joseph was delighted at the prospect of opening the hamper earlier than he had expected. Owen was curious to see St. Anne's; he had lived all his life in Blexton, and he had never seen any of the ruins. Norma appeared nervous about traveling the overgrown pathway and even more nervous about the choice of a stopping place. She timidly questioned the advisability of trespassing on such haunted ground.

"My lady," she ventured, "might we not wait a bit for a clearing after the turn? A nice place is sure to be found after we turn west."

"It's quite all right, Norma. At least we'll know we're safe in such a secluded place."

"Well, yes, ma'am. I guess we can but hope we don't get lost in these woods."

Caroline was firm in her decision to stop at St. Anne's. The party had no choice but to dismount and lead their horses through the undergrowth in silence. When they arrived, Joseph set about finding a spot clear enough to spread dinner. Then Norma busied herself with the hamper, with bread and knife, avoiding any comment or notice of their surroundings on the edge of the gray stone compound. Owen found suitable places to tether the horses, looking around him in some awe, wanting to ask questions, but deciding against it. Caroline said she would walk around a bit on her own and join them in a few minutes.

"Is that wise, ma'am?" Norma asked. "You could take Owen along with you."

"No, I'll be all right. I won't go far."

She wandered to the gray outline of what must have been a dormitory. The convent was very small; judging by the size of what had to be their sleeping space, there couldn't have been more than half a dozen nuns. She found two or three outbuildings at the rear and what must have been the small refectory. It looked as though the kitchen and the warming room shared the same space — probably the chapter meetings had been held there, too. The convent must have been very poor. Some distance behind the kitchen Caroline found a ground vaguely squared — it must have been the kitchen garden. She saw a vine of tiny green pearl-like clusters about twenty feet away — a grapevine. It was still alive and growing, still bearing fruit.

She had put off the sanctuary until last. But she stood there now and faced an altar, white marble grained in green, broken and lying on the ground, covered now by moss, and made holier by being broken.... Once it had been anointed with chrism, consecrated, the place where — how many times? — the great miracle of all the ages had happened. The place, the site, where humble earthly bread became the very flesh of God.

In front of the altar and to its left, sunlight filtered down through the leaves of the overhanging oaks, still young, growing now in the place that must have been the small choir, making it seem even more light-filled than it would have been had there been no trees there now in place of singing nuns. It was beautiful beyond bearing. Had it been more beautiful when it was alive? When it was inhabited by nuns singing praise to God seven times every day? How could it be, though it surely was so, that this silence now was more beautiful? Whatever had been the aim of the king's men, they had not wiped out the small convent's beauty when they smashed its windows, broke its altar, burnt pictures, books, and then the sanctuary itself. They had only made it more beautiful than its own builders could have dreamed....

The emptiness of it all was so strangely full—like its silence, so deep that it was full of sound. Everything, every place in the ruin, was full of its own contradiction, like two worlds existing together, in the same space, at the same time. How could that be? It was as though there had been a sketch over which a contradictory overlay had been placed in an attempt to eradicate it. But that hadn't happened. Instead, the two realities existed together, and instead of the intended contradiction, the overlay had made something else altogether. Destruction had been transformed into creation—its intention notwithstanding—and it was a creation greater, more beautiful, than the reality it meant to destroy. Destruction had succeeded only in making it eternal.

Standing there among the weeds and saplings from the overhanging oak trees, in the middle of the sanctuary, Caroline recognized the experience. It wasn't a frightening sensation, not even a strange one. It had happened to her once before, and she remembered it now. It happened when Father Joseph had placed the Blessed Sacrament in a monstrance on the altar in Thompson's house. Each of them—all the Anders family, Thompson, and she herself were to take an hour's turn in watch during the night. Her hour was midnight. And Caroline remembered. It was as though—she could never find words for it—as though the universe had become somehow *too full*. She could not remember her hour ending, could not remember John touching her on the shoulder where she knelt on the floor—the universe was too full. There was no room in it for John's touch, no room in it for anything else at all, not even for her. And yet—she knew all the time where she was, she knew the hardness of the bare wooden floor under her knees, the sharp smell of the burning tallow of the candles, the hunger that assaulted her belly and stayed there. She knew the pain that shot through the small of her back, running upward through the muscles to her shoulders, shoulders that ached, that felt as if they were broken. She knew it all. It was *not* as though she had been transported somewhere else, to someplace other than where she was. She knew it all—all of it—and yet she knew nothing except the Sacrament on the altar, until Father Joseph came and knelt in front of her, speaking gently, telling her that sunrise had come, that it was time to say Holy Mass.

Turning to her right toward the choir, she saw the young stranger who had shared their table at the inn. He was a few hundred yards away on a small brown horse, riding into the treeless sunlight some distance from the far side of the small compound. She watched him; he was leaving, going away....

Just then, she felt a sudden grip of her arm as Norma came up behind her.

"My lady! It's him!"

"Yes, it's him," Caroline replied.

"He is following us!"

Caroline turned to face Norma. "He is leaving. He was here before us. It's more likely that we are following him." Then she noticed the fear on Norma's face. "You're afraid of him, aren't you?"

"Yes, ma'am. I am."

"But why? Last night he behaved with great respect—with kindness even."

Norma looked puzzled for a long moment, looking toward Stephen. Then she answered slowly, "That's why, my lady."

Stephen was gone from their sight when Caroline looked back. They returned to the horses and the men. Caroline thought about Norma's answer, how strange it was—and even more about why it didn't seem strange at all.

6

The evening of the same day, May 24

Thompson was walking on the road near the Johnson farm. He had not given up hope entirely that Eleanor and Charles Johnson would return safely, but his doubt had increased with each passing hour, and now it surpassed that hope. Grief crowded the edges of his heart as tears crowded the edges of his eyes, waiting to rush in, to flood him in sorrow. He had walked the perimeter of Andersgate, no longer able to pray. In a way, he handled trouble much like Margaret. As she walked in the forest when she was troubled, he walked the estate, and today it seemed he was walking every inch of it. He could not be in the presence of John or Margaret back at the house; there was no longer any way he could hide his anxiety.

His position at Andersgate was unique; he was both servant and family. Andersgate maintained a fairly sizable staff, some twenty in all, and all of them lived on the estate. The only Catholic among them was Thompson, originally retained by John's father many years ago when they were both very young men. Thompson had been a groom for a family in York who ran afoul of a government investigation of York Catholics during the reign of Edward Tudor and lost all their holdings, keeping only their lives. Ben Anders had been in York on business at the time and brought Thompson back with him to Andersgate as his stable manager, and he eventually became steward. He had never married. He lived in unusually large quarters for a single man, a house on the estate that had been built for the previous steward who had a family. He lived there alone and refused to allow any of the maids to clean or cook for him. He ate nearly all his meals with the family. None of the servants had ever been in his house. It was regarded as a very mysterious place.

The remainder of the servants were non-Catholics, a matter of more than a little inconvenience for the family, but the wise decision of Ben Anders. That circumstance precluded any scrutiny of the family by unfriendly outsiders, but apart from that, it forced them to be habitually cautious. No rosaries, crucifixes, prayer books—nothing was ever left lying about or stored in some convenient drawer or cupboard where it might be seen by an attendant. And as the habit of caution pervaded their daily lives, it was easier to be cautious in the village or anywhere away from home. Many of their fellow Catholics who were recusants condemned secret Catholics like the Anders family, believing them to be apostates. Yet, as persecution of the recusants grew, so did the number of those who chose to protect themselves from the suspicion of informers and the scrutiny of government spies. Only Thompson knew how many there were in Somerset, and that number was much greater than anyone would have imagined.

The Anders family had lived on this same relatively small estate in the hills of Somerset, next to the ancient Forest of Dean, for over two centuries. The first "Benjamin" among them was Judah Benjamin, a Jew from York who converted to Christianity fifty years before the Jews were expelled from England during the reign of Edward I, in 1290. Though Judah was a Christian by then, and married to a Christian woman, with children and grandchildren, he was deeply affronted by the false charges made against the Jews of counterfeiting money. The real reason for the expulsion was that the king and several noblemen owed them money. The law forbade the loaning of money by

Christians, so that occasional necessity was consigned to Jews. When debts mounted, some cause for expulsion was created, the Jews' property confiscated, and they were forced from the country. The same thing happened to Jews repeatedly all over northern Europe. King Edward had been less cruel than most; he had allowed them to keep the cash they had, but he had seized their property and, of course, the debts that were owed to them. Though Judah was well established as a Christian in the village of Kefington by that time, the expulsion caused him to promise himself that his heirs must maintain the name of Benjamin.

But Judah Benjamin's only son had no male heirs. His eldest granddaughter, Hilda, had married an Anders. To honor her grandfather's wishes, she named her son Benjamin, and since that time, all male Anders children had Benjamin as one of their names. It was Hilda Anders and her husband, George, who had bought the original acreage that later grew to become Andersgate. There were farms attached to the land, but the family income had never consisted merely of tenant farming or sheep herding. Very early, the Anders had begun buying wool and selling it to merchants outside the district. Eventually, that trade grew until it became, under Ben Anders, a large exporting business of other commodities. Now, under John, it had diversified still more and had expanded to many parts of the continent and even across the sea to the colonies. Though there was no outward appearance of it, the Anders family had become very wealthy.

None of the family had ever been involved in public life. Past the expansion of the estate to include a few farms a hundred years ago, the size of their property had remained comparatively small. They had never had a strong taste for luxury, and they preferred to live very quietly and simply, with only family and close friends as visitors. Andersgate was secluded, situated so that it could never be discovered even accidentally by some traveler. One would have to approach it quite deliberately from the single narrow road that led to it, south of the village of Kefington.

Except for the compulsory Sunday services at the parish church, visits into the village were fairly rare. Only Margaret went into the village often. That was one reason Eleanor had been an ideal messenger: she could be absent from home as often as necessary and few of the folk in the surrounding area even knew she was away. And there were paths through the forests surrounding Andersgate that only the family knew. When Eleanor was not accompanied part of the way by Thompson himself, the Johnsons' son always went with her. The Johnsons were the only Catholic family on the Anders farms, so knowledge of the paths was kept to a minimum. On this trip, she had taken Charles Johnson with her, a sturdy lad of seventeen who always leapt at any opportunity to ride as protector of Mistress Eleanor, whom he not very secretly adored.

Thompson had visited Mr. and Mrs. Johnson that morning and stayed with them through the midday meal. At first, they seemed to be taking great care to appear unconcerned about the long delay in Charles's return, but Thompson knew better. He finally said to Edna Johnson, "I know how worried you are—" but before he could say more, the woman broke into sobs. Her husband put his arms around her and tried to comfort her.

Thompson had half-expected anger; he had expected them to blame him as the one responsible for whatever may have happened to their son. Instead he had been humbled by their courage.

Patting his wife's back while he held her, Mr. Johnson said simply, "Mr. Thompson, we know that if anything's happened to our Charles, our loss would be no more than your own." And Edna Johnson, her face buried in her husband's shoulder, swiftly nodded her head. Thompson had found it difficult then not to burst into tears himself.

He was not a philosophical man, nor even a particularly religious one. He had no identity independent of the Anders family and no purpose outside their protection, prosperity, and happiness. He was of the same stuff as great soldiers, sworn to protect, conserve, and defend; great monarchs, for the same reasons—and even great saints in his capacity for devotion. Apart from his love for her, Eleanor's death would be hard for him precisely in this way: it would be a contradiction of everything dear to him; and thus walking the perimeter of Andersgate was for him a recalling of his purpose, a recalling of that for which he lived each day of his life.

Now he paused and stared into the sunset in the west behind the house; he knew he had to return, had to face Margaret, had to acknowledge that, yes, something must be wrong—terribly wrong. But just as he paused and took in a great breath, preparing to turn toward the house, he saw a figure rising above the knoll on the road from the southeast. His heart stopped. *Could it be Eleanor and Charles?* But no—no, it wasn't. It was a man he didn't recognize, followed by a woman— Caroline Wingate's maid. He recognized her in her muslin cap and gray woolen gown—then Caroline, followed by a boy, or a small man—he couldn't tell at this distance—leading two packhorses. Instead of the pleasure he would have felt by Caroline's arrival, his heart seemed to drop to his feet. Not just because she wasn't Eleanor, but because it seemed to Thompson that Caroline's arrival was a confirmation that comfort for Margaret would be needed; that grief was now certain; that, any moment now, the dreaded news would follow. It was with no haste that he went forward to meet them.

* * *

It was well before dusk that evening when Stephen reached Compton Lane, not far from the western gate of the ancient bustling city of Bath. He held Stella's reins in his left hand as his right hand lifted the rusted iron knocker on the door of the small house. Ellen MacDonald answered his knock.

"Hello, ma'am. I am here to see Mr. Farwell. My name is Stephen Long."

"Oh, welcome, sir. We've been expecting you. Let me get my son Samuel to take care of your horse." She yelled back into the house, "Samuel!"

"Oh, that's kind of you, ma'am, but I'll take care of her, if you don't mind. She's not mine, you know, and she's had a few days of hard travel."

"I know, sir. As you wish. Here's Samuel. He'll help you." A cheerful husky young man of twenty years or so arrived and took Stella's reins, smiling at Stephen and patting Stella's neck.

"This way, sir."

Stephen followed him through the narrow passage beside the house to a small stable, not more than a shed actually, with two stalls at the back of the house. Another horse was there, Farwell's own, most likely. "Well, Samuel, I see your horse is well tended. I'm sure that Stella will be too."

"Oh, yes, Father. We'll be taking old Bob here to Andersgate tomorrow."

"Andersgate? Where is that?"

"I think I'd best let Father Farwell tell you about that. If you'll go through that door there, you'll come to the kitchen. My mum will let you in."

Stephen noted Samuel's use of the title *Father* and said, "I take it, Samuel, that you and your mother are Catholic? I know that she is the housekeeper."

"My mum is, I'm not—Catholic, I mean—but yes, she's his housekeeper for many years now, since my dad died." He paused a moment, then added, "But don't be thinking I'm the queen's disciple, Father. I'm no dissenter neither, though I go to

Her Majesty's Sunday service like everybody does, if they know what's good for them."

"England is having hard times, Samuel." He slapped Stella's rump to help her turn in the stall.

"Oh, aye. Whether the hard times last will mostly depend on the English, I reckon. But she's fattening them up quite proper on 'Englishness,' and people like that stuff, you know, Father."

Stephen thought young Samuel might have more wisdom than his years should bring. He smiled. "I'm sure I will see you later, Samuel."

It was Father Farwell himself who greeted him at the door, hand extended. "Come in, come in, Stephen. I did not get a chance to meet you before you left for Douai, but I knew your parents—fine people. Please follow me into the study. Mrs. MacDonald," he said over his shoulder, "can you bring us some warmed wine, please? Would you like that, Stephen?" He was using two canes to walk, leaning heavily on both; walking was clearly painful for him.

"Oh, very much, thank you." Stephen followed him along a close hallway to his tiny study, which held a single narrow window to the passage he had just walked with Samuel and Stella. The priest was old and frail, he noted, and he was trying to rouse the fire in the small hearth, balancing on one of the canes. Stephen took the poker from his hand. "Here, let me help with that, sir."

Father Farwell sat down carefully in one of the two chairs facing the hearth. Stephen pushed the top log aside to allow the flame of the lower log to rise and catch. Then he sat down in the other chair, holding his hands to the fire, thinking that there was no sound as welcome as a crackling new fire on a cool English evening.

"Now then," Father Farwell said, leaning toward him. "Did you have a safe crossing?"

"Yes, sir. Very safe. There were no problems at all in the crossing. And the Braithlows were very kind and hospitable to me. I was well cared for, though, as you know, they weren't prepared for me. I only hope it won't cause them trouble. Enough evil happened because of my arrival." Suddenly he felt his eyes well up with tears. It was good to be able to say aloud what had been unspoken, even in his mind. "Those people—the escorts—were there in that farmer's barn on account of me—and the Braithlows' sons barely escaped with their lives."

"That's not altogether true, Stephen. Francis Braithlow told me all the details when he brought the awful news. They were not in that barn because of you. If Taversley had remained at the cliffside, as he should have done that night, they would all have been safe. But he'd been instructed to watch over the farmer's bull, and the escort, instead of staying at the tavern, as they should have done, decided to pray a Rosary in the farmer's barn with Taversley. They should not have taken such a risk. It's not your fault, Stephen. They had gathered to meet you, yes—and Taversley was to bring you to the tavern after your arrival at dawn to meet Eleanor Anders. Then she and young Charles Johnson were to bring you here. But their decision to pray at the Leacham farm the night before was not your doing—it had nothing to do with you."

He made no further remarks to assuage the guilt Stephen was feeling, thinking that the less discussion of it, the quicker it would be overcome. "But I have other unhappy news for you, personally," he said. He wore a sad little smile. "Father Joseph Tidwell of Somerset was arrested and taken to the Tower in London last week, whence, I am sure you know, he will not return."

That news was unhappy indeed, but Stephen also sensed that his plans were about to be changed for him. "Is there no hope?" he asked.

"None. He was arrested while he was saying Mass." He placed his hands together and bowed his head, closing his eyes. "He has had a lifetime of serving our Lord, and he is a very old man, even older than I." His voice was soft, almost inaudible. "I know him well, and I know that somewhere in himself, he rejoices in the opportunity to suffer for the Lord and for his flock. Even in such a horror as that which lies before Father Tidwell now, our Lord gives his peace, if we surrender that suffering to him and offer it to him in reparation for the offenses of ourselves and others. Joseph Tidwell has done so, I am sure."

He raised his eyes and laced his fingers, resting his elbows on the arms of his chair. "But this means that the western part of Somerset is left with no priest at all now, while the eastern part—where you expected to go—already has two." He watched the young man's face. He knew that Stephen had not seen his family for six years while he was away at the seminary in France. He knew that his family was eager to see him, to make certain he was safe. He expected some disappointment, but he saw none, only comprehension, like the arrival of expected news—though this news could not have been expected. The gray eyes were at peace.

"Yes, sir. You send me to the west." It was a statement almost perfunctory, not a question.

"I am afraid so. You will be very much needed there." His smile became a little apologetic. "It's a beautiful county, you know."

Stephen tried to smile in return. "Do you think I could get word to my family?"

"Oh, certainly. I'll see to that. And, after all, when some time has passed—a few months, perhaps—you'll be able to get away for a while to visit them." He thought it would be many months indeed, with only one priest in all of western Somerset and so many Catholics. Almost half the population of that district was

Catholic, either recusants or secret Catholics, and at once he thought with sadness of the Anders family.

Mrs. MacDonald arrived with cups of warmed spiced wine, to Stephen's great pleasure. The scent of cloves rose in small wafts of steam as he held the cup to his lips. The old priest watched the young man. He was so young — probably not more than six-and-twenty — and his slight boyish body seemed lost in the coarsely woven brown tunic, provided, no doubt, by one of the much larger Braithlow sons. He had a close-trimmed short brown beard and short brown hair, an expression like any ordinary young Englishman, a student perhaps, nothing extraordinary at all about him, except perhaps for his eyes — gray, like a calm sea over unfathomed depths of power. He felt a real affection for him and hoped that Stephen would learn to love the people of the hill country in the west. Severe as they sometimes were, they were very devout, and many had suffered much under the queen's hatred and fear of the Church. He put aside thoughts of the letter he must give to Stephen to deliver and for the moment enjoyed his visit with him by the fire, sipping Mrs. MacDonald's fortifying spiced wine, talking of mutual acquaintances in France, of the political turmoil there, of the Devonshire weather, of Somerset and its people. He found himself simply taking pleasure in the ordinariness of this young man. After a time, however, he perceived in Stephen a mounting need for expression of something personal. "You look troubled," he said.

Stephen hesitated but then gave voice to his anxiety: "Sir, I am fearful."

The old man leaned back in his chair and sighed. "Of course you are," he said.

"But I should have no fear," Stephen protested. "I should rejoice to do God's will, to suffer for the faith, as you say Father Tidwell does. I must confess this...." He looked as contrite as a child.

"No, no. You shall make no such confession, Stephen. I am sure that if he is still alive now, if Father Joseph rejoices, he is also full of terror. He is a man, Stephen, just as you are. Listen, he told me some years ago that he reads St. John's account of Gethsemane every day. It reminds him that our Lord himself desired not to suffer, not even for his Father's will. Never deny your own humanity, lest you deny the same humanity of our Lord." He saw that Stephen struggled with this admonition. "Hold your fear close to your heart, even cherish it, for that is where you share our Savior's Cross—not in his divinity, but in his humanity, in his Gethsemane." He was relieved to learn that the young man was no zealot, that he had the good sense to be frightened—it would make him cautious.

"But he died willingly, with his own will, for the sake of the Faith."

"Did he? Did he die for the sake of the Faith, Stephen?"

Stephen didn't answer—the question was a strange one.

Father Farwell's eyes almost closed as he watched Stephen's face. "Did he die for faith—or did he die for love?"

Stephen sat immobile, looking down into his cup of wine. He didn't answer. The quiet, gentle question of the old priest brought something like a small, sudden light in a dark place—it was unexpected. He felt himself becoming aware that there had been something cold and hard, like ice, inside him, which now seemed to be melting. He would think of this question later, meditate on it, understand it … maybe answer it; for now, he was silent. And because it was a question unanswered, the silence lasted a long moment, while Father Farwell watched his face, his downcast eyes.

Then the old priest leaned forward in his chair. "Now," he said firmly, "I must send with you a letter to the families of those in Somerset whose children were martyred in Devon. Because I know how worried they must be about the fate of their loved ones, there should be no delay in informing them of this evil news. That means there should be no delay in your departure. I think you should leave very early tomorrow morning, after you've had a good night's rest. I'm sending young Samuel with you to Andersgate. It's the safest house in Somerset, and it's where you must deliver the letter. Samuel knows the way; he's been my messenger to Andersgate several times before."

* * *

At about the same hour that Caroline was making her arrival at Andersgate, Edward sat down to a cold supper at Somerfield. He had not begun to eat when he heard the sound of a great many horses on the gravel just below the dining-hall window. His heart sank as he rose to get to the door before Alice, who had already arrived there before the loud knock came. "I'll take care of this, Alice. Go back into the house."

"Yes, sir," she mumbled, her eyes wide.

Bentwood stood on his doorstep, and in darkened silhouette against the brilliant sunset, several men on horseback remained mounted. One of them was Robert, whose face he saw only in profile; he kept his face straight ahead and did not turn to look at Edward. He was holding the reins of another horse on which sat a man, his hands bound behind him, his shirt hanging down in shredded bloody tatters from his whipped and still-bleeding back; his face, beaten and swollen, hung down on his bare chest.

Bentwood spoke from a wide smile, revealing a row of beautifully straight white teeth, his good cheer in macabre contrast to the scene behind him. "Good evening, Captain Wingate, sir. Sorry to trouble you, but we will be requiring your signature on this order for the execution of Josiah Braithlow, traitor to Her Majesty's government. The man has confessed to harboring a popish priest on his farm." He spoke rapidly, providing details unasked for. "We have not harmed Mrs. Braithlow at all, sir, though she clearly played a part in the crime. Her Majesty's law is always merciful wherever possible. The woman is ill, dying anyway from the look of her—though where she'll do her dying now, I do not know, since this man has forfeited his property to the Crown by his treason. The two sons fled into the forest, but they had no horses and were on foot. My men will find them soon enough." His smile remained.

Edward stood in the doorway, struck dumb. He kept looking at Robert, willing him to turn and face him, as if he were looking for some explanation, some expression of remorse, *something*, but Robert kept his face averted.

Bentwood said, "Sir?" His brilliant smile disappeared, and he looked through narrowed eyes at Edward. "Harboring a Catholic priest is a capital offense. You might want to call your servant to bring a pen?"

"Oh, yes. Of course," he said, averting his own face. "Alice!" he called over his shoulder in a voice suddenly strange and thin to his own ears. "Bring a pen from my desk."

"Yes, sir." She bustled into the hallway and out again, returning with the pen, while Edward avoided looking at the hunched figure on horseback. He took the pen from her and pulled the door almost closed behind him, feeling that here was a sight no woman should see, not even a servant.

Bentwood was smiling again. His good cheer nauseated Edward. He held out a document, which Edward pretended to read, then placed it on a small polished board of oak that he had held tucked under his arm, a board designed, apparently, for this purpose. How often was this same scene taking place throughout the country?

He held the board outward toward Edward, keeping the fingers of his gloved left hand on top of the document to hold it steady. "You will be pleased to know, sir, that we have struck gold here in your little village of Blexton. Because of this one arrest, we have not only the name of this priest—who was hidden in this traitor's barn on the twenty-first of May—you may read the particulars in the order for execution if you so choose—but also his destination when he departed on the twenty-third. The house of still *another* priest in Bath, name of Farwell, I believe. Two birds with one stone, what? As soon as this distasteful affair is concluded in the morning, you may be sure that several of Devonshire's brave militia will be on their way to that house in Bath."

Edward glanced up at Devonshire's "brave militia"; not a single man was known to him. On the contrary, they were all foreign mercenaries—Rhinelanders, from the look of them. It was no wonder that a new tax had been levied; such mercenaries were not cheaply come by. He scrawled his signature, noticing as he did that below his signature line were the words, "Magistrate, by appointment of Her Majesty's Council." As soon as Edward signed, Bentwood snatched the board and tucked it back under his arm. With gloved hands, he rolled the document and tapped it against the front of his black velvet cap, which was adorned with a brooch of gemstones, and smiled brilliantly again. "Thank you, sir," he said. "We will handle everything from here. Good evening to you." He had already turned to mount his horse.

Edward took a step backward into the hallway. "Good evening," he mumbled, though Bentwood had not waited for a reply. He closed the door and stood there facing it. He did not want to turn, to go back into his house again, to his supper, to his life. But he knew he must, and so he did.

7

Stephen woke to a light tapping on the door of the small bed-chamber where he had spent the night. Mrs. MacDonald's head peered around it. "Father! It's time to wake up." She held a candlestick and extended it forward. "Can you dress in the dark, or do you need a candle?"

Stephen stirred himself with some difficulty; he had slept very soundly. Mrs. MacDonald's pork pie at supper, the wine, the wonderful conversation with Father Farwell after a day of travel — all the hospitality of the house had so relaxed him that he had gone to sleep immediately. "No," he said, "I can manage without the candle."

"All right. Samuel is already saddling the horses; he'll meet you in the street. I packed a hamper for you and a jug, so that you can stop for breakfast when it's daylight." She turned to leave but changed her mind. "Oh," she added, "please don't feel slighted that Father Farwell will not be bidding you farewell. The poor man needs his rest, and I decided not to wake him. Likely he'll be cross with me for that."

"No, no, that's quite all right. He gave me his blessing last night. He should rest." She closed the door softly, and he pulled his tunic over his head and struggled with his boots. Then he put the letter addressed to the Johnson and Anders families inside his tunic. Below stairs Mrs. MacDonald was waiting at the street door. He could hear the horses' hooves tamping softly on the cobbles. She opened the door to the darkness outside; there was just enough light to see Samuel already mounted on the gelding and holding Stella's reins. Steam issued from the horses' nostrils into the chilled air as the gelding whickered softly, ready to go.

Mrs. MacDonald leaned her nightcapped head out the door. "Samuel, you will be careful, you will do whatever Father tells you, and you will return safely to your poor old mother."

"Yes, ma'am," he said. "I shall be back on Monday—likely afore supper."

"What about Stella?" Stephen asked.

"Unless somebody there needs a ride back, I'll lead her back here," Samuel answered.

"I know Farmer Braithlow needs her. She's all they have."

"Don't worry, sir. She'll get home."

"I don't suppose I'll have a horse in Somerset," said Stephen.

"No, sir. No place to stable one without suspicion. Afraid you'll do most of your traveling there on foot."

Stephen had already begun to understand the extent of a priest's dependence on the faithful. He would have no "home" but would be a guest in whichever home he entered, just as the Lord had instructed his apostles when he sent them forth to announce the Good News to the world. All he owned—including the items needed for Mass—would have to fit in a knapsack. Total poverty would be the circumstance under which he lived, and total dependence would be his way of life.

He mounted his horse, and Samuel leaned down and kissed his mother farewell. The shuttered windows of the nearby houses were so close, Stephen knew that in spite of their attempts to speak low, the neighbors must have heard their voices.

The horses' hooves clattered on the deserted cobbles as they rode slowly toward the western gate. When they turned the corner, Samuel picked up speed and the noise increased. "It's not good to have so much coming and going from the house," he explained. "We can go a bit faster now we're away from it."

"Samuel, didn't the neighbors hear us as we left?"

"Yes, sir. Likely they did." He smiled at Stephen and added, "But as Father does often say, you don't have to be a good Catholic to be a good neighbor, sir."

The comment warmed Stephen's heart in the chill of the early morning air.

They had ridden more than five miles before the sun rose. Stephen was enjoying himself, already finding in Samuel a comfortable companion. He wanted to ask him to stop referring to him as "sir." There was little difference in their ages, probably only five or six years. There was a vast difference in their education, of course, but Stephen knew that Samuel's formality of address was due to his priesthood. It made him realize how lonely this new life would be. But after the loneliness of yesterday's travel, Samuel's companionship was very welcome. He found himself rapidly developing an affection for the young man as Samuel's humor and lightness of heart affected his own mood, which seemed to move always somewhere between a vague fear and a firm resolve. He wondered why Samuel wasn't Catholic and decided he'd approach that subject when they knew each other a little better, when he could be sure that Samuel wouldn't be embarrassed by the question.

Only when he thought of the letter he carried did his spirits sink, and he decided to stop somewhere and spend some time in prayer before delivering it into the hands of the families who would, he knew, receive it like a knife in their hearts. And to make the news even worse, they would not be receiving it from old Father Joseph, whom they knew, trusted, and loved, but from him—a stranger to them and the bearer of the worst message they would ever hear. He knew there were no words of his that could lessen the pain he would bring, but he wanted to pray and ask our Lady in particular to help him—she who knew so well the grief that these mothers would feel, both Mrs. Anders and Mrs. Johnson.

He thought about the tragedy that his return to England had meant—even before he actually arrived—and remembered the stormy weather, the barren rocks. But the image of the little blue cornflower sprang into his memory like a candle dispelling the darkness around it. It was not the first time. It seemed now that each time the heavy questioning—*why am I doing this?*—hammered his heart into that darkness, there was an appearance of a kind of blue quickening, which he had come to recognize as the flower that had greeted him among the stones of the Devonshire coast. Yet, as consistently as it visited him, it never occurred to him that it was the answer to his question.

Meanwhile, he was finding in Samuel—whom he had begun to call Sam—the beginning of a friendship. Somewhat tentatively, Sam had begun to ask him questions—about priestly celibacy, sacraments, the papacy, among other things.

"I couldn't ask Father Farwell, you know, though I know he'd have told me, but he would've wanted to catechize me, you know," Sam laughed. "He's a dear old man, and good to my mum and me. Without his taking us in when my dad died, I reckon we'd have been begging in the streets of Bath now."

For his part, Stephen learned much local lore and gained much information about Father Joseph, the Anders family, and about a girl in Bath named Doreen. He learned how beloved Eleanor was by her mother and her brother, John, and by old Thompson, the steward of Andersgate. "Now, Father," Sam had said, "Mistress Anders is not like my mum. She doesn't ever think with her head, but only with her heart. I tell you true, I fear what this news will do to her. Mr. John has a lady friend in London named Mary Posten, and I reckon that she'll be the next Mrs. Anders. I do wish she was there now. Or even better—Mistress Caroline, her niece. Mrs. Anders seems always happy and peaceful when she's about."

Stephen decided to put off thinking of his letter until he stopped to pray and to enjoy the journey with Sam until then. Sam told him that they would reach the Johnson farm about half a mile before they came to the main house, the home of the Anders, and so they planned to stop a mile or so ahead of time, to allow Stephen some time to pray and to prepare himself.

* * *

In Blexton, Josiah Braithlow was hanged for treason at sunrise. It was all over before anyone knew about it. Indeed, the only native of Blexton present for the execution was the sheriff. He had sent for Edward to be present, but when the rider came and woke Alice, and she went upstairs to wake the magistrate, Edward had sent word that he declined to attend. Now, it was all over.

The marketplace buzzed with no other topic. It seemed that half the people of Blexton had sudden recollections—things that were now seen as strange goings-on among the recusant Braithlows. At The Three Lions, half the patrons "always knew" and the other half declared they "should have known."

Everywhere there was an unbearable dearth of information. Questions flew every which way, but the only sources of real information were absent: Captain Wingate—the new magistrate who had judged Josiah—would not come into town, nor would the sheriff. The militia had already departed—headed north toward Bath, most people said, on the trail of the popish spy and other traitors Josiah had named in his confession. In the absence of information, rumors became facts. Somebody said that Simon Leacham had come upon a whole nest of spies in his barn; others said he had somehow been in on the capture and questioning of Josiah, but no one knew any details about that.

Before noon, however, the important facts were known, Mrs. Lewis having provided most of them. It was reported that Mrs. Wilson—who could believe it? The rector's wife—had paid a sick call on Mrs. Braithlow and had spotted a popish priest lurking around the barn. Just what a priest should have looked like was not discussed, but everyone was certain that it was only Mrs. Wilson's loyalty and sense of duty that had made her inform on the recusant farmer.

"For I know her well," said Mrs. Lewis, "and nothing else could have made her do it. She's that tenderhearted, you know."

Everyone stayed far longer at the market than they had intended, not only to gather and share the news, but in the hope that Mrs. Wilson herself would arrive. Patricia was staying at home, however. Andrew had forbidden her to leave the house, and she was torn now between her chagrin, caused by his command, and her triumph—which so filled the house that it seeped under the door of Andrew's study, making it impossible for him to concentrate, even if there had been no other, more compelling reason for his lack of concentration. He had gone to his study and opened the commentary as usual, but he could not read. A shadow appeared between his eyes and the page. It would not go away. Indeed, Andrew would never read his private collection again. The cupboard where it was stored remained locked forever afterward.

Meanwhile, Patricia's dignity and vindication grew so large as to assume a stature that filled the house, finally to a point past bearing. Andrew relented and went to the drawing room to give his permission for her to go to market. It was the last time Andrew ever gave permission to his wife; after that day, she never required it again. He retained his authority in the pulpit, but in his home, there had been an irrevocable shift.

Now between the cabbages and the onions, she said to the cluster of goodwives who surrounded her at the market, "What

I want to know is why poor Captain Wingate has not shown his face—and what's more important, *where is Mrs. Wingate?* She usually comes to market this day. My Betty said something this morning that she'd heard from someone at Somerfield: *Caroline Wingate has fled.* And what I want to know is, *why?*"

It didn't take much for her hearers to supply their own answers to that question, and though the answers differed slightly in their details, the general conclusions were the same: Mrs. Wingate had somehow been in on the conspiracy, and poor Captain Wingate was ashamed to show his face. Everyone wondered aloud what would come of that situation. Just when they realized that they would have to wait to hear what would happen, fresh news arrived from Somerfield—Captain Wingate had dispatched letters to Sir Arnold, to the captain's family seat in the Midlands, and to London. Was he planning to leave Devonshire?

* * *

At Andersgate, everyone slept late; there had been much talking and dining the night before. Thompson alone had risen early and departed without breakfast. Owen and Joseph had received some minor assignments from him, after which they were free to walk into the village and visit the tavern. The Anders staff was too large as it was, so there wasn't much work to be given them; Norma, however, remained behind. She unpacked and tended Caroline's wardrobe and personal things, as well as her own, but she was feeling a little offended now because Caroline had sent her below stairs, saying that she wanted to spend time in private with her aunt and cousin.

The air indoors seemed unbearably heavy at breakfast. John went into his study after breakfast, while Caroline and Margaret took needlework to the garden. They sat under a cluster of yew trees at the northern end. Margaret had given Caroline the embroidered coverlet on which she had been working for the past year; she had brought the mending basket for herself.

At supper the night before, Caroline had learned of Father Joseph's arrest. She was grief-stricken; she had known him almost all her life. Because of her grief, the others had been reluctant to mention their fears for Eleanor. But Caroline knew that something was wrong besides Father Joseph's arrest, and she suspected it was Eleanor's delayed return. She decided she must bring up the subject herself.

"Aunt Margaret, when should Eleanor have returned?"

"I could not say for sure, dear. Thompson has told us that she was unexpectedly sent from Bath to Devon in order to meet a new priest there and take him back to Bath. She should never have gone on so dangerous a mission, but, since there was no one else, it could not be helped—or so Thompson says." She paused a moment, then added with some contrition, "And I know it's true—Father Farwell would have used Eleanor only as a last resort."

"To Devon? Oh, I wish I'd known … but I could not have seen her anyway.…"

Again the air was heavy with unspoken words, unacknowledged anxiety. They plied their needlework in silence for a few minutes more. Then suddenly Margaret spluttered: "Even so, she should have returned by now!" Caroline heard the anger at the edge of her aunt's fear. "And no one will mention that—not John, nor Thompson either! Yet I ask you, do they think I am a fool?"

Caroline grasped Margaret's hand. "I think, dear Aunt, they do not wish to alarm you until they are certain there is cause. Don't be angry with them."

Margaret withdrew her hand and reached into her sleeve for her handkerchief. "I do know that, Caroline, but the silence is deafeningly loud, you might say." She dabbed at her eyes a moment. It was good to have the words out at last, but now she felt a little ashamed of her anger; she knew John and Thompson wanted only to protect her from as much worry as they could.

Caroline sensed Margaret's guilt—a feeling that afflicted her far too often. "Don't feel badly, dear. It's very painful to be obliged to suppress our feelings, regardless of the motive for doing so."

There was silence for a moment while they resumed their needlework. Margaret glanced at Caroline's face; its softness had hardened around the mouth—a beautiful mouth that had been made to smile always. The corners of her lips were turned slightly downward, and she could tell now that the expression had become permanent. Consumed by her own anxiety, she had not noticed how Caroline's face had changed since she last saw her eight months ago. Whatever news of Eleanor might come—any moment—whether it was bad or good, nothing for Caroline would change. Nothing *could* change. At least, in the enforced deceit they all had to share, Margaret was able to love John and Eleanor openly and fully. But even if Caroline had children, she would not be able to love them as she should, as she would want to love them. For how could she love her children and raise them to hate the Church? How was that possible? Yet it would have to be so. Caroline had to live every day within the prison of her Protestant marriage, with no children to lighten her heart, and—oh, what of the nights? Her loneliness must be unbearable. Of all people she knew, Margaret thought Caroline suffered most, for she knew her niece well and understood her—her very soul was created for obedience. How did she bear it? Margaret looked at the pain that had gathered at the corners of Caroline's eyes. She was aware more fully than ever of how grave a sin her brother William, Caroline's father, had committed in marrying her to Edward—and in the name of love he had done this to her!

"Dearest Caroline," Margaret whispered, "how can I counsel my own counselor? I cannot, but I can ask you, how would you speak to someone else in your position?"

Caroline flinched as Margaret took her hand. Then, taking a deep breath, she said, "What would I say to someone like me?" She almost smiled. "I would say, 'Have faith. The Lord will give you an answer.'"

"Well, there you are, my dear." Margaret started to pat her hand, but seeing the look on Caroline's face, she thought better of it. She dropped her mending, rose, and stood behind her niece's seat, embraced her shoulders, and leaned down toward her. She spoke softly through the soft brown curls into Caroline's ear. "Do you have your rosary?" Caroline nodded. "Well, then," said Margaret. "Mine stays in my mending basket. Come now. Hold your sewing in your lap and keep your hands low. No one will see."

* * *

The road had begun to rise and fall more than it had before, and Stephen realized they were reaching the hills that surrounded Andersgate. The sun had long since passed its zenith and was directly in front of them now as they rode westward. The air was warm and clear, the sky cloudless. To his right the southern end of the great forest loomed, dense and deep with tall evergreen trees, making a wide dark band between the green fields and the blue sky. As Father Farwell had said, it was beautiful country, peaceful and fertile.

Samuel rode beside him. They had been silent for a long while now, their conversation having become increasingly less frequent as they made their progress westward toward a destination neither of them wanted to reach. The letter inside Stephen's tunic became heavy and almost like a living thing. A narrow lane appeared now, veering off northward, and Sam stopped.

"Father, this is the road to Andersgate," he said. "I reckon we're about a mile from the Johnson farmstead."

"Let's stop as soon as we can now, Sam. We can finish off that bread and ale from breakfast. Then I'd like a little while alone, please."

"Yes, sir."

They turned into the lane and rode a little farther until they spotted a pleasant spot, where they dismounted. Sam started to take the small hamper down from the back of his saddle.

"You can finish it, Sam," Stephen said. "I'm not hungry." He took his rosary from his kit and looked around him for a suitable place to pray. "I'm going over to that cluster of stones under the oak tree there to pray a Rosary," he said. "I think we can use some help especially from our Lady in what we must do."

"All right, sir. I may doze off a little when I've done eating. Just wake me when you're ready to move on."

Stephen settled himself on the ground amid the stones with his back against the oak tree. He took the letter from his tunic and read it again. Father Farwell had made no introduction of him in the letter, and for that, Stephen was grateful. The families did not need to be informed about who he was—they would know—and any secondary purpose in the letter for the sake of mere form would have been to diminish its single import. It was brief, and it made no attempt to lessen, to soften in any way, the message it conveyed. To do that would have been hurtful, and the message itself was hurtful enough.

Stephen made the Sign of the Cross over the letter and replaced it inside his tunic, took up his rosary, and began to pray.

* * *

It was well past the dinner hour when Thompson, nearing the eastern end of Andersgate on horseback, heard Edna Johnson's scream. He pulled the reins and stopped, frozen for a moment, knowing nothing and everything at once. Then he spurred his horse to a hard gallop toward the farm. He arrived to see a number of people in the yard before the cottage door. Edna was in her husband's arms; both were sitting on the ground. A few workers and neighbors stood in groups, embracing each other and crying. Sam MacDonald was there with a young man whom Thompson didn't know. Sam stood behind him, hugging his elbows, as the young man sat on his heels on the ground facing the hysterically screaming woman and her husband. Thompson knew the young man was the new priest.

As Thompson entered the yard, he swallowed the shards of his own shattered heart. He spoke quietly to Sam: "I know, don't I, Sam?"

Sam nodded, turned aside from the others, and whispered, "Yes, sir. It was Sunday night, sir, in Devonshire. It was in the barn of a man named Leacham. They were saying a Rosary with John Taversley, a workman there. It was a pistol, sir."

Thompson knelt behind the shaking shoulders of Charles Johnson's father and held them from behind. "Oh, God, Allen, I am so sorry."

The young priest seemed to have forgotten caution; he was holding Edna's extended hand and speaking prayers in Latin. Thompson whispered to him, "Careful, Father." Instantly Stephen ceased his verbal prayer. He made the Sign of the Cross in Edna's palm and held it to his lips, then stood with Sam and waited for the bereaved parents to pass their shock before he would try to get them alone in order to read Father Farwell's letter to them. Presently one or two of the workers drifted off, and he whispered in Allen Johnson's ear. Johnson began urging his wife to her feet and steering her toward the open door of the cottage.

The shade from overhanging trees, the advent of late afternoon, and sorrow itself darkened the room. A woman lit some candles as she choked back sobs, then took Edna Johnson's hands and held them to her breast. "I'm going now, dearie, but I'll be just outside. You call out if you need me." Then she left through the open door as Allen tried to lower his wife into a chair. As she sat down, new wails of grief erupted, and Stephen grabbed both her hands and held them tightly. "Mrs. Johnson, try to hear the words I read, I beg you." Thompson saw that the young priest's own cheeks were wet.

"Hush, Edna," her husband was murmuring. Sam sought some water and a towel. Stephen took advantage of the lull in weeping to read Father Farwell's letter:

My dear children in Christ,

As you read these words, you already know of the martyrdom of your son and daughter, Charles and Eleanor. There is nothing—no words I can say—to ease your pain. I know that. Even now, as I write these words, Father Joseph is enduring an agony unimaginable to us. And throughout our country—who knows how many suffer the same grief as your own, even perhaps this day, this hour. This is not the first time or place in the history of Holy Mother Church that her children suffer, nor shall it be the last. Why does it happen? Why did the Cross happen? In the end, these are not two questions, but one. And we must accept our share of the Cross now for the sake of the sovereignty of God, just as he gave his own Son's life for the sake of our salvation. Know now that you yourselves are martyrs as well as your children, and trust in God, for he well knows your pain. And last, know that my own heart breaks for you, that you are ever in my prayers and never more than now.

Yours in Christ,
Clive Farwell

As Stephen folded the letter and replaced it in his tunic, Thompson turned to him and introduced himself as the steward of Andersgate. He said, "I take it, Father, that you go now to Mrs. Anders and her son?"

Stephen answered yes, but he wanted to remain there with the Johnsons while he felt his presence was helpful. Mrs. Johnson still clung to his hand and showed no sign of letting go. He turned to Mr. Johnson: "The lady who lit the candles—is she still nearby?"

Mr. Johnson said, "I'm sure she is." He crossed the room and put his head through the cottage doorway, where several people still stood nearby. "Ethel," he said, "could we have your help with Edna, please? We want to get her into bed if we can."

The woman named Ethel bustled inside and followed Thompson and Sam as they lifted Mrs. Johnson and carried her to her bed. Then she fetched the pan of water and the towel that Sam had readied, sat by the woman's bedside, and began bathing her face and hands. The men left the room. Sam started a fire. Johnson slumped into a chair, holding his head in his hands. It was then that Stephen really noticed Thompson for the first time. He was standing next to the doorway, his hands hanging at his sides and his forehead against the wall. He approached him. "Mr. Thompson, Samuel told me about your situation with the Anders. She was like your own daughter, sir, was she not?"

Thompson could not answer. He felt as though he were dead. How long he stood thus he did not know, but presently, he turned to see that Sam was standing next to him. Stephen was sitting with Johnson in chairs close to the hearth, talking in very low voices. Two women were in the bedroom with Mrs. Johnson, and a third was busy preparing food. It was almost dusk. Thompson knew John and Margaret would be worried about him; he had not been home all day. Sam followed him to the two men sitting by the fire.

Stephen stood and spoke to Thompson in a low voice, "I have just told Mr. Johnson that I wish I could stay with them tonight, but I must also go to the main house." Thompson winced. "I am gratified to see that they have such good Christian neighbors, but I will return early tomorrow morning for a private Mass here, with them alone. You may wish to come with me, Mr. Thompson?"

"Yes, sir," Thompson said, "of course."

"We should go on now to Mrs. Anders and her son." Then he turned back toward Mr. Johnson and shook his hand. "I will see you tomorrow, sir, and hold you in my prayers tonight."

"Thank you, Father." Johnson murmured.

Thompson followed the priest and young Sam out the door. The sun was down, and it was growing dark. The three men mounted their horses and walked them slowly as they headed down the winding lane toward Andersgate.

They were silent for a long while. Then Thompson stopped, causing Stephen and Sam to stop as well. He turned and faced Stephen, as if struck by a sudden realization. "Father, it cannot be a coincidence. No. There is one creature on earth I would wish to be with Mrs. Anders and John now, and she arrived yesterday evening—Miss Caroline, Mrs. Anders's niece. It is no accident that she came—just now, just at this time."

They continued then, with Thompson talking about Caroline and how she affected Mrs. Anders and everyone at the house. It relieved him to speak thus, to talk of matters not directly related to what lay ahead of him and behind him, as though the slow progress toward the house were removed from time. If only the journey could last, never end, and they would never arrive.

But arrive they did. And John saw them through the window on the upstairs landing. He knew Samuel, he guessed who the stranger was, he knew why Thompson was late getting home, and he knew his sister was dead. He raced down the stairs to be with his mother before they reached the door. She and Caroline were still sitting in the dining hall when he burst through the door. "Mother—" he began, as if he would somehow shield her from what he knew was about to happen. Margaret stood slowly, her face white, as the sound of the horses on the gravel outside reached their ears. John rushed to her and held her in his arms as the muted noises of the men's arrival came to them from the hallway. No one spoke. They were standing, facing the doorway, when the men entered.

Thompson came through the doorway first, followed by Sam, and then the stranger. Caroline gasped when she saw Stephen. For just a moment, they stared at each other in a mutual shock of recognition. She knew too much at once. She knew that Eleanor was dead, she knew the stranger was a priest, and more—more that she could not have named then. None of this knowledge was comprehensible, only stunning. And so she stood frozen, not even obeying the instinct to breathe, unaware of Margaret as she crumpled sideways, falling into a heap of crimson wool and white lace on the floor at her side. Finally, she blinked her eyelids and breathed, as she knelt quickly beside her aunt and grasped her into her arms, holding her close to her bosom, rocking her like a child.

John faced the three men, his back to his mother, and stood rigid, his face flushed with rage and his hands clenched into fists—as though he would strike the first man who dared to speak. As shock struck the room into paralyzed silence, it was only Thompson's face, as he stood mute by Sam's side in the doorway, that expressed the wordless truth—a grief beyond bearing. But he took charge. Within the hour, Margaret was upstairs in her bed, and her personal maid, Eloise, and a housemaid were shuffling in and out of the room, bringing warm water, towels, changing Margaret's dress to a fresh shift, warmed by the fire. She had not yet regained consciousness and Caroline sat by her bed, holding her hand in both her own, praying softly over fingertips that were ominously tinged with blue.

Below stairs, the men sat near the hearth in the drawing room with strong wine. John had just finished reading the letter from Father Farwell. He started to hand it back to Stephen, but Stephen said, "You should keep it, Mr. Anders."

John gave him a rueful half-smile. "We can't, Father," he said, and threw the letter into the fire.

"No, I suppose not," Stephen replied.

"Tell me, Father, is it because of you that my sister is dead?" John looked at Stephen directly, challengingly.

"No, no, John," Thompson stepped forward and answered him. By then he had learned all the details of Eleanor's death from Sam, and he related them now to John, tenderly, patiently, as a father might try to calm an angry son.

"I'm sorry, Father," John spoke in a whisper.

"Please. It's all right," Stephen answered, placing his hand on John's shoulder. "I am so very reluctant to say this, but it must be said, John. Given the way that so many of our brothers and sisters have had to die, try to see God's mercy: Eleanor's death was swift, with no suffering—and she died in the midst of prayer." And it was only then that John's rigid self-control left him, and he leaned forward over his knees, placed his face into his hands, and wept like a child. At the same time, Margaret regained consciousness upstairs, and all of Andersgate heard the piteous wail of a mother, as if she were holding her dead child in her arms.

8

Andersgate lay too still, in an unnatural silence. Caroline woke to find herself still seated by Margaret's bed, her head resting on her arms. Soft gray light crept around the edges of the shutters. Margaret moaned softly from time to time, but at least she was sleeping, restless though her sleep was. Caroline watched her aunt's unsteady breathing. She knew that no hour of the day is more cruel for those who grieve than dawn, and she prayed that Margaret would sleep at least past this hour. She pressed her palms against her eyes. She was alone now for the first time to hear her thoughts, but she wasn't sure she wanted to be. News of Eleanor's death had not been a surprise — not to anyone, really, including her — but it had the effect of blowing open a door of dread that had made all thought of anything else impossible. Now, memories of Eleanor flooded her mind — the two girls playing together in the garden as children, with toy horses, running together in hide-and-seek from John. She pressed her hands tighter on her eyelids. There would be time to remember, to grieve, but for now, Aunt Margaret needed her presence of mind.

In the silence of these moments alone, she thought of Stephen. She knew him now to be the new priest — but who was he, really, and where did he come from? Again, as she had at the inn, she felt that she knew him. He appeared to be as shocked as she was when she saw him in the dining hall last night. It was clear that he understood as little as she; there would be no point in asking him. And there were things so much more important to cope with now—perhaps later, if there was an opportunity for such a conversation. But just the thought of him now in these moments alone brought her peace, making her feel tranquil and strong.

She stroked the back of Margaret's hand and kissed it lightly, then stood very quietly and straightened her back. Margaret's servant Eloise lay on a cot across the room, snoring softly. Caroline shook her shoulder gently and whispered, "Eloise, I'm going to my room to wash. I'll be back shortly."

"Yes, ma'am." Eloise swung her legs over the side of the cot. "Can I get you some breakfast, ma'am?"

"No. Wait here until I return and stay with Mrs. Anders in case she wakes. Then you can have cook make some porridge. Maybe we can get her to take some later."

"Yes, ma'am." She rose to take Caroline's chair by Margaret's bed as Caroline went to her own room, where Norma slept.

Norma had been saddened by the news of Mistress Eleanor's death, but she was also gratified to be needed again. As far as she and the house servants knew, Eleanor and Charles Johnson, who had been her escort on a trip to Bath, had been set upon by robbers almost two weeks ago. One or two of the servants openly wondered why the bodies were not returned, but then they satisfied themselves that it was probably because the bodies had only just been discovered after such a long while, and it had been necessary to bury them straight away, likely in the churchyard at Bath. And likely it was this young man, this Mr. Long who came with Sam MacDonald, who had discovered them. It wasn't long before they had figured it all out. As they ate their breakfast around the long table in the kitchen, they talked about how this Mr. Long must have come upon the bodies and then gone into Bath to find someone who could identify them. Having found Sam, the two of them must have returned for the bodies and buried them in Bath. Then Sam, likely, had brought Mr. Long with him to Andersgate to notify the families—and probably also to answer any questions the families might have. The narrative they made by talking together was somewhat complicated, but it seemed sensible to them.

"Oh, just think how dreadful it must have been," the upstairs housemaid said to the others in the kitchen, "Mistress Eleanor and young Charles gone ever so long—and they could have been killed on the very day of their departure from Andersgate. How dreadful. It's a wonder—" She didn't finish her thought. Everyone knew it was a wonder the bodies had not been preyed upon by wild animals. There was a stunned silence then, as each of them wondered if perhaps they had been, after all.

The housemaid's audience was attentive. Mr. Thompson had not yet made any announcement to the staff, and because it was she who had been instructed by Thompson last night to prepare a room for Sam and Mr. Long, she was closest to what little information they had at that point. Neither Mistress Anders's maid Eloise nor Caroline's Norma had appeared below stairs yet. They would have more information then, perhaps. Meanwhile, no one could determine what their duties were, whether they should go about their normal tasks. They felt that, until they heard from Mr. Thompson, there was little they could do except sit around the large kitchen dining table and wonder, and comment frequently on what a grace it was that Mistress Caroline was in the house just now. Finally, Eloise appeared in the doorway from the back stairs.

"Mistress Caroline says you should make some porridge," she said to the cook, Maybelle, who rose instantly and started giving orders; it was such a relief to have something to do.

Thompson had slept in John's room, neither of them wanting to be alone that night, and he woke now while John still slept and dressed quietly in the dim light of dawn. He had told

John the night before that he, Stephen, and Sam would be going early to the Johnson farm to say Mass and that they should return by midmorning. He closed the door softly and found Stephen and Sam already waiting for him on the landing. The three of them descended the stairs together and left by the front door while the servants talked together in the kitchen. They walked the half mile to the Johnson farm, where candles were burning and Edna and Allen Johnson awaited them.

* * *

When they returned around midmorning, Margaret had been persuaded by Caroline to take a few spoons of porridge, then she cried herself blessedly to sleep again. After a breakfast of porridge and bread in his room, John moved between his mother's room and his study. He dismissed Richard for the day, and though he did no work, he found his comfort there among his papers, moving from his desk to the window, where he stood staring down on his mother's gardens for long periods. All the servants were sent below stairs except Norma and Eloise, and an unnatural quiet lay over the entire house, as though it were deserted. Joseph had gone to work in the fields, finding the atmosphere at the house unbearable. Owen remained in the stable all day. By midmorning, he had curried the horses until they refused further attention. Now he set about oiling the tack. He felt a sharp sense of danger to his mistress now, and his instinct made him want to keep all in readiness for immediate departure from this place. Meanwhile, he found what peace he could as he always did, among the sounds and smells of horses and hay.

The return of Stephen, Sam, and Thompson from the Johnson farm provided some relief from the dismal, ghostly pattern that had been set by a house in deep mourning. Stephen went to Margaret's room, and Eloise was dismissed. She went below stairs and reported in whispers to the servants, "I think Mistress

Anders wants details now of all that he found and what happened. Oh, I do not think such a course is wise just now. I do hope Mistress Caroline persuades her to wait a bit." And the servants clucked in sympathetic agreement, but they all remarked what a kind young man this Mr. Long must be. Poor though his cloth was, he was truly a gentleman. They wondered aloud how long he would stay before returning to Bath.

No announcement or instructions from Mr. Thompson had been forthcoming, and the cook said that on reflection, she wasn't surprised about that. The poor man had loved Mistress Eleanor as though she were his own daughter. They had much to speculate about, and the kitchen became a hub of whispered fragments of news and observations. In the absence of any instruction, the cook decided that soup and bread were in order for dinner and set about making the best marrow soup she could, while her helper made fresh bread. Molly busied herself in her dairy, declaring that a soft mild cheese and fresh butter would be nourishing and comforting at this time. But they all stopped and noticed when they saw through the cellar window Mr. Thompson taking Samuel MacDonald into his house. The purpose of that extraordinary event was a topic for almost a half hour before one of them suggested that maybe Sam would receive a reward for his pains. This possibility remained a satisfactory explanation until someone else wondered: Shouldn't the young man, obviously so poor, also receive a reward? Yes, likely he would, when he had done with Mistress Anders's questions, of course. It was therefore no surprise when, an hour or so later, Thompson was seen emerging from his house, Sam having apparently stayed behind, and then returning after a bit with Mr. Long by his side. They were sure he was taking him into his house where he would receive a very handsome reward. Eloise dispatched young Edgar, the cook's ten-year-old, to the stable. "Tell Michael to get their horses ready," she told him. "They will likely be departing for Bath soon now." But though she kept an eye on the window between her little tasks for Maybelle, no one emerged from Mr. Thompson's house.

* * *

Sam had been in Thompson's house before. He knew about the inner room. The walls inside the house had been removed and a single interior room constructed in their place. There were no other rooms in the house except Thompson's office on the left in the front and his small bedroom on the right. There were two beds in Thompson's bedroom; one had been used by Father Joseph when he had visited in the past. Because there were no windows in the interior room, candlelight could not be seen from outside the house. The room was surrounded on all four sides by a narrow passage. Access to the passage was gained through a door at the back of Thompson's bedroom, but the door to the square inner room was on the opposite side of the house, at the back of the passage. The room could be entered only by that door, which bolted from the inside. Once inside Thompson's house, the inner room was not difficult to find; the plan had not been to conceal the room so much as to delay access to it. Because of the solid walls of both the room and the passage, candlelight was required even during the day.

Against one wall of the room stood a bare table, which became an altar at Mass. Above the table hung a large crucifix of chased silver with a golden Corpus. On either side of the table, there was a half wall of books. The only furniture besides the table was a prie-dieu six feet in front of the table. There were some plain, straight wooden chairs stored against the wall at the back of the room. The family stood during Mass, except when they knelt one at a time on the prie-dieu to receive Communion.

While Sam held a candlestick, Thompson removed one of the books from the bookcase to the left of the altar-table, and an open latch was revealed. He steadied the bookcase on its fragile hinge with one hand while he swung it open with the other. A small room was revealed behind the bookcase. When the draft from the dark room had passed, Sam handed the candlestick to Thompson.

"We've never had to use this for aught but a sacristy, Father, so I've not put a bolt on the other side, but here, let me show you." Raising the candlestick in front of him, he lowered his head to lead Stephen through the doorway into the little sacristy room. Stephen drew in his breath sharply. On one side was a shelf holding golden candlesticks, a chalice, a ciborium, a paten — all glittering in the candlelight — and a beautiful folded lace altar cloth. There was also a small wooden box full of fresh candles.

Seeing Thompson genuflect toward the ciborium, Stephen genuflected also, then asked in surprise, "You have consecrated Hosts here?"

"Yes, Father. Always." He did not mention it, but he thought again of how wonderful it was to sleep under the same roof where the Blessed Sacrament reposed. He had thought often that he was as blessed as a monk might have been sleeping in a dormitory next to a monastery sanctuary.

Opposite the shelf, on the other side of the tiny room, a suspended rod held an alb, stoles, and gold-embroidered vestments of white, green, red, violet, and black.

Stephen touched a white chasuble embroidered in gold and red. "They're beautiful, Mr. Thompson," he said. "How in heaven's name did you acquire them?" He was genuinely amazed; he had never seen vestments so rich and lovely before, not even at the seminary in France.

"Oh, I didn't do it, Father. Mr. Anders did all this many years ago. We have always had Mass here whenever Father Joseph could come. He would hear our confessions on the Saturday — maybe you'll be hearing them this afternoon, Father?"

"Yes, of course. We can say Mass tomorrow morning."

"That's good—Mrs. Anders may be up and about by then, I think."

Stephen agreed. "She'll want a requiem Mass for Eleanor as soon as possible, I'm sure."

"Yes," Thompson said. He made a mental note to set up the chairs. He didn't think Margaret could stand for the Mass. "Anyway, when Father Joseph came," he continued, "he'd hear our confessions, and then we would have Mass here the next morning before light. Now let me show you how he came and went." He held the candlestick to the rear of the sacristy, and it sputtered in a draft. Stephen looked down to see a flight of steep wooden steps. "At the bottom is a narrow tunnel, Father Stephen. It leads all the way across the pasture to an opening at the foot of Gaston Hill in the forest. Father Joseph always used this way to keep from being seen in the daylight at Andersgate. Mr. Anders built it for escape, but thank God, Father Joseph never had to use it that way. Wherever he was when he was arrested, it's a shame there was no escape such as this." He turned his back to the dark passage and faced the inner room, where Sam stood waiting. "In the early days, when it wasn't so bad, the priest could come and go at the house in the daylight—but not anymore. Too dangerous now. The servants of Andersgate are good people, but—well, I don't have to explain, do I?" He paused and sighed sadly.

"Yes, I understand," Stephen murmured. He saw himself in the future, arriving here from the tunnel, opening the unlatched bookcase door, and preparing for Mass. He knew that after tomorrow's Mass, whenever he came to Andersgate, he would stay in Thompson's house and never see the main house again.

"You stay here always, Father, for as long as you need to, and as long as you can. It won't be that often, though, and it won't be for long. I have messengers who'll tell us when and where you're needed anywhere in Somerset—and it's a big country here, you know. You'll stay busy, Father, and I'm sure you know that you'll never be out of danger anywhere, but at least here at Andersgate, you're probably as safe as it's possible for a priest to be nowadays in England."

Thompson led Stephen back to the interior room. "When Mr. Anders and I built this many years ago, things were not as bad as they are now. He meant it only for escape, and I confess now that I thought he was being overcautious. But now—well, if anyone discovered this room, they'd know what it is. And they'd probably find the tunnel right away—unless the latch was closed and there was someone here in the room at the time. Then they'd think they had caught their prey, maybe, and not go looking further."

Stephen looked at Thompson's face, so set in earnestness as his voice trailed off. He realized that Thompson had made a plan in case Mass was ever discovered, a plan to make intruders believe "they had caught their prey." The delay that would be caused by the way the house was constructed would give Thompson the time he would need to pull a chasuble over his own head, push Father Joseph into the sacristy and close the latch—so that the intruders would believe they'd caught their priest. He knew that Thompson had never revealed this plan to Father Joseph—just as he wasn't revealing it to Stephen now.

Thompson looked around at the room and made a small rueful smile, thinking that the elaborate construction was now naïve. "Maybe someday none of this will be necessary."

The three of them were quiet for a moment—none of them believed that "someday" would ever come now. "When this queen came to the throne, there was still some hope," Thompson mused. "It could have gone either way then. But not now. It's too late now, even if she changed her heart. The Scottish queen's claim—"

Sam interrupted him. "It's simple, sir—not hard to figure at all. The only weapon the queen's got against the Scottish claim is to keep the English in a fever of hate for Catholics, to make folks as scared of them as she is." Sam's bluntness, the inarguable plainness of his point, was not lost on Thompson or Stephen. "She's got Queen Mary in prison now, anyway—and you can know for sure that she'll never leave that prison alive."

Stephen sought relief from the depressing silence that followed. "Well," he said, "I don't know if you know about the new Society of Jesus. They're sending missionaries to England—"

"We know about the Jesuits, Father," Sam interrupted again. "They're not missionaries; they're just fresh meat for the queen's butchers. She calls them foreign spies, but they're all of them as English as you and me."

"Well," Thompson broke the silence that followed Sam's dismal view. "Here, anyway— We're very much out of the way here." He turned to Stephen. "I think, for this time, Father, we can let it out amongst the staff that you and Sam are staying here in the house with me, and you won't have to use the tunnel, of course. It will seem a little strange to them for you to be staying here instead of in the main house, but I suspect they will explain it to themselves somehow by the special circumstances of your presence. They know you're here, and they think they know who you are, so everything will be all right."

"Very well, Mr. Thompson."

Stephen walked around the bare wooden floor of the room and looked at the bare walls. No stained-glass windows, no lovely tapestries or marble, yet the room seemed truly a sanctuary. Before they closed the hidden passage, Thompson took a purple stole that hung across the rod, folded it, wrapped it in a length of homespun, and gave it to Sam to carry to the house. Stephen would need it when he heard confessions in his room later that afternoon.

They returned to the house. Watching from the cellar window, several servants saw Sam carrying a homespun bag they were sure was full of money, a large reward for him and Mr. Long to share. Sam and Mr. Long continued into the house, but Mr. Thompson came into the kitchen.

"Oh, Mr. Thompson," the cook said, "I've a lovely marrow soup ready, if anyone is willing to take it."

"Thank you, Maybelle. I'll go see what the family wants to do about dinner. I'll have some myself, in any case. It smells wonderful. I'll be back in a few minutes."

"Yes, sir."

He went first to John's study, but not finding him there, he went to Margaret's bedroom and knocked lightly on the door.

Caroline answered. "She's asleep again," she whispered, "but come in." There he found John sitting in the chair beside the bed; Stephen and Sam were also there.

"Maybelle has some soup ready and wants to know if anyone can eat," he whispered.

But then Margaret opened her eyes and looked around her. Caroline, John, Sam MacDonald, and the new priest were all there in her bedroom while she had been sleeping. John's eyes were swollen, and Caroline's were laden with fatigue. For the first time, she became aware that her sorrow was making the sorrow of others harder to bear.

She sat up and said aloud, "I am not asleep, Thompson. And I will have some soup as well. I must get up and dress now. Tell Maybelle we will have dinner in the dining hall, not in this bedroom."

"All right," Thompson said. With Margaret awake and whispering no longer necessary, it seemed to him that there was a break in the near-unbearable pall of grief that blanketed the house, and even if it would last only for the dinner hour, that would be a very good thing.

But dinner was a somber affair. No one spoke much because the presence of the servants made any real conversation impossible. When dinner was over, Eloise came into the dining hall to ask Margaret if she wanted her to have a fire kindled for them in the drawing room.

"No," Margaret answered. "We will go back upstairs. Please tell Maybelle that the soup was very good. We will have it again for supper if she has enough of it, along with some cold meat and a bit of fruit."

"Yes, ma'am. She'll be pleased." She made a little curtsy and turned to leave.

"And, Eloise," Margaret stopped her. "Also, please tell everyone to remain below stairs. We want to be left alone for the rest of the day. Make sure you also inform Mistress Caroline's maid."

"Are you sure, ma'am? I could wait on the landing in case you need—"

"No, I'm certain. Some of us have had little rest." She looked down the table at Caroline. "We'll be taking a nap for a while."

"Yes, ma'am."

When Eloise returned to the kitchen, everyone thought the information was good news—a nap now was just what they needed—except Norma, who was noticeably disappointed by the request for her absence. Eloise understood the desire to be of service, to be needed, so she said, "Norma, maybe you can help me do some of the washing." And Norma agreed; it was better than doing nothing at all to help.

Upstairs, John sat in the chair by the cold hearth again in his mother's bedroom. There had been no opportunity to talk with Stephen since the night before, when he had delivered Father Farwell's letter. Sam knew Stephen by now, of course, having spent the last couple of days with him, and Thompson too had spent some time with him, but John knew nothing about him. He had watched the young priest at dinner—and Caroline.

They sat opposite each other at the table, yet neither ever addressed or even looked at the other. John thought that was odd, and the oddness was compounded now in his mother's bedroom, where everyone was present. Caroline stood by his mother next to her bed as she was getting ready to lie down, and the priest was across the room by the window—yet they seemed oddly close. He was aware of the presence of intimacy. He was about to dismiss the feeling when Caroline turned from Margaret's side and John could see his mother's face. He was surprised to see how his mother was looking at the priest—he could see that she also felt the same mysterious presence.

As it turned out, conversation was no easier in private than it would have been in front of the servants, simply because everyone was too exhausted. Margaret suggested that Stephen go to the room where he had stayed with Sam the night before and prepare for confessions there. They could each go to confession there one at a time and then rest until supper. She knew that some of them, especially Caroline, had rested far too little, and Mass before dawn tomorrow would mean a very early rising. There would be plenty of time for conversation tomorrow after Mass—which would be celebrated as always before daylight.

"Wait a minute, ma'am, not just yet," said Thompson, thinking more clearly than Margaret was able to do. "I'm afraid we have to decide some things now because of the horses. Father has a horse with him. We need to figure out how to get the horse gone while he stays behind in the house." He thought Stephen looked very tired, so he added, "And I'll do my confessing later—at the house. After you hear the family, Father, you could rest till supper."

"The horse problem's easy," Sam spoke up. "While Father is saying Mass before daylight tomorrow, I can leave with both horses. When dawn comes and the servants wake up, you can tell them that Mr. Long and I already left for Bath."

They agreed that the plan was a good one, though Stephen believed there would be enough time for Sam to go to Mass before leaving. Even though Sam wouldn't receive Holy Communion, it seemed important to Stephen that he attend Mass.

Meanwhile, Margaret saw Caroline sway on her feet and knew she needed to lie down right away.

"Father, if you would go along to your room now, I'll send Caroline for confession after a few minutes. Then she can lie down on her own bed and get some sleep."

Stephen nodded and left to go to his room. Since there were no servants upstairs then, it would be easy to move along the hallway quietly, one at a time. When he had said his prayers, kissed the purple stole, and placed it around his neck, Stephen opened his door to find that Caroline was waiting. She was very pale. Neither of them had spoken of their first meeting at the inn. It was as if they had both decided that topic was too unimportant now in the presence of grief; it could be mentioned later, perhaps when the grief had subsided.

There was no screen for privacy in confession, and Stephen didn't know what he should do. "How did Father Joseph hear confession with no privacy?" he asked, feeling awkward.

"He was always in Thompson's house," Caroline answered, "and we just made our confession there before Mass."

"What about privacy? There's no screen there either."

"Father, privacy is a luxury that we cannot afford. We are lucky to be able to confess at all. There are so many who have no chance."

She was wondering if they would speak of their earlier meeting at The Rose and Thorn now. She wanted to tell him that she had seen him at the convent of St. Anne. In fact, it was that moment, when she had seen him riding away in the sunlight, that returned to her when he arrived in the dining hall the night before and she knew him to be a priest. It had stayed with her constantly since then. It seemed to have meaning; she wanted to tell him about it, to talk about it with him.

"I suppose I can sit here," he said, going to a chair in the corner of the room. "You can get a pillow from the bed for kneeling."

Caroline got the pillow and placed it on the floor in front of the chair, thinking of how fragile, small, and incongruous Stephen looked in his coarse brown tunic with the purple satin stole around his slim shoulders. He looked like a little boy playing at being a priest.

He sat in the chair and made the Sign of the Cross over her as she knelt on the pillow before him. But Caroline didn't speak right away. She had been dreading this moment. She had always dreaded making the same confession to Father Joseph—but it would be worse with Stephen. The new priest didn't know her and didn't know her life, but there was another reason. The prospect of self-revelation to this man—to whom she had felt such a strange response, one she did not understand, filled her with something more than dread—almost like a sense of foreboding. An upward glance at his face made that sense even worse, for it seemed he felt the same fear.

Finally she mumbled, "Father, I deceive everyone, and I deceive my husband."

"Everyone has to be deceptive now, Caroline. That is no sin you must confess. But how is it that you deceive your husband? Is he Catholic?"

"No," she answered, "nor does he know that I am."

Stephen was surprised. Every marriage, he knew, was unique, but a husband's ignorance of his wife's faith would be an odd marriage indeed. "Tell me the circumstances of your marriage," he said.

She told him everything then. She told him about her desire, ever since she was a child, to enter a convent in France. When her mother was alive, it was understood that she would leave as soon as she came of age, and she had lived in happy anticipation of taking the vows she had long since made in her heart. But after her mother died, her father would not let her go; instead, he insisted that she remain in England with him, and he arranged what he called a "safe" marriage for her, to someone who was not Catholic. Certain that the prospective bridegroom, the respectable son of Sir Thomas Wingate, would not marry a Catholic, her father made her promise to keep her faith secret. Caroline knew that her husband held no anti-Catholic convictions, but that was because he held no convictions of any kind. Like her father, she knew Edward would not tolerate her faith, not because it was Catholic, but because it was not socially and politically acceptable. She told Stephen all this without bitterness or rancor, without resentment. Given her father's purpose in selecting a husband for her, there could have been no better choice than Edward Wingate. Moreover, she added, Edward was a good man, a man who would make a fine husband for any woman.

"I see," said Stephen, sharply aware that, though Caroline had made no mention of it, her own wishes in the matter had been disregarded. The entire purpose of the marriage had been to assuage her father's grief, and Caroline herself, probably from an instinct to obedience, had apparently made that purpose her own as well. He looked above her head toward the window behind her. *Ah, Lord, your bride was taken from you.* He looked back at her face, marked by unreflective suffering, and sighed for her. She was in pain. Aloud he said, "All right, now confess your sins," though he wondered what sin such a creature could confess.

Caroline bowed her head and mumbled, "Father, I am a poor wife. I do not make my husband happy, and Edward is so good. He deserves to be happy." She waited for the same penance Father Joseph always gave her: pray a Rosary to our Lady and ask for the grace to make her husband happy. She had prayed many such Rosaries.

But Stephen asked, "How are you a poor wife, Caroline? Do you think your deception makes your husband unhappy? I could assure you that it's not so."

Keeping her eyes on the floor between them, she blushed and drew a deep breath. Father Joseph had never asked a question so personal or direct. "No, Father. It's because … because I do not please him."

"How is that? Why? Why is he displeased with you?"

Her voice was barely audible. Stephen had to lean forward to hear her. "I do not desire him," she answered. A knot had formed in her throat, making speech difficult.

Stephen sat back in his chair and closed his eyes. Of course you don't, he thought, how could you? His manner of hearing confession was not just to hear the words of the penitent, but also to hear what the penitent did not say, what the penitent himself might not be able to say. He thought now of the guilt she had endured, and the helplessness. But more—and so much worse—the desolation. It would only deepen as long as her life with her husband continued as it was. If she were truthful with her husband about her faith, the barrier to intimacy might be removed, though her husband might well divorce her. But even if he did not, that confession to her husband, by itself, would remove only the guilt of her deceit. It would not remove the guilt of *despair*, a sin far more grave, but one she could do nothing to remedy as long as it remained unacknowledged … too painful for her to see, because the estrangement from her true Spouse was unendurable for her.

"Do you have children?" he asked her.

"No, Father," she replied.

He looked at her bowed shoulders—not the effect of travel fatigue, as he had thought when he saw her at the inn. Of course, she couldn't give her husband her desire—she had none to give. She had been compelled to disavow her own—in order to satisfy the desires of others. And she was left empty, with nothing left to give, save her obedience.

In another time, another place, this denial of her human dignity could not have happened to her. The laws of the Church would have protected her from a marriage without her consent, a marriage without the blessing of her own priests and bishops—a marriage outside her Faith. But in the darkness that now swallowed England, all manner of moral confusion ruled. It was not even clear whether Caroline was bound by such a marriage. An inquiry would be a superfluous indulgence now, when a Catholic soul must struggle merely to survive.

Stephen looked down at the woman who knelt at his feet, her head bowed, her eyes downcast, confessing the guilt of not pleasing the husband she had never wanted. Her own holy virtue of obedience had been her undoing in a world where obedience had been turned upside down, where the authority that should have saved her had been used against her—by those who claimed to love her. Stephen longed with all his heart to lift her up, to raise that bowed head, to restore to her the life she had been denied, the joy of hearing the voice of her beloved as he called to her, of answering that call. But he could not.

"What do *you* want, Caroline?" he asked.

She looked up in surprise. "I want to die," she answered simply, surprising herself by giving voice to her most private thought.

He closed his eyes and groaned within himself, silently. The gift she had once had to give—her love, the dowry of her heart, was gone, squandered and ravaged in this forced and unblessed marriage, like the forced marriage of England itself. He prayed: Was there no hope for her now? Was there nothing he could do? He opened his eyes again and looked at her, feeling all her brokenness within the brokenness of his own heart.

The long silence of the priest made Caroline glance up at his face, but she quickly lowered her eyes again. She had the feeling that he was looking *through* her, past the barriers of her body, to the depths of her soul. For a fleeting moment, she felt as though she had been invaded, exposed. And with a suddenness that made her gasp, she realized that feeling meant that something must still be there, that something within her must still be *alive*.

Stephen sighed. Caroline's lashes lay against cheeks as pale as death. No. There was nothing he could do for her now. She would have to continue as she was in this barren and brutal marriage, in exile from her own desire, from herself, and from the love to whom she belonged. He breathed a wordless prayer in which he offered her to God then, for he himself was helpless. He opened his palm. He had been holding a small crucifix while he heard her confession.

"This is love," he whispered and held the crucifix out to her.

She straightened, rising from sitting on her heels to an upright kneeling position. She had sunk into a void that felt almost like a peaceful oblivion, emptied of words that had been a forgotten burden on her heart. Now she gazed at the figure in Stephen's open palm, hearing the words he had just spoken, *This is love*, echo into that void. She kissed her fingertips and touched the crucifix. The emptiness was filled with a sudden and piercing longing to know what this meant. She looked up at Stephen's face, but the gray eyes held only a calm gentleness, revealing nothing—nothing at all.

She fell back on her heels again, thrown back on herself to find his meaning. And there—there, something stirred. Something that had been dead was awakening—something wonderful. And Caroline seized it. It was not any kind of meaning at all that Stephen had given her—what he had given her was *herself*. She almost felt faint with the weight and the wonder of it. For just a moment, tears came to her eyes, but they did not fall. No. There had been enough tears. The time for weeping was past.

He said softly, "Now say the Act of Contrition." She did. Then he absolved her of any sin with the Sign of the Cross and said in a voice barely above a whisper, "Go back to your room now. You have no penance."

"Yes, Father." She rose, unsteady on her feet, but full of certainty and a strength that was new and strange — and wonderful. She straightened her shoulders and walked to the door, then turned to find him looking after her. "Thank you," she said.

"No," he whispered. "Thank you."

She closed the door quietly behind her, and as she left, all of Stephen's self-doubt left with her, like clouds that had been hiding a light too bright, revealing that which he was not sure he wanted to see. His false humility was exposed, as was the endless self-questioning with which he had hidden its falseness from himself. Yes, he was where he was meant to be, doing what he was meant to do — and whether he would suffer and die for it had clearly never really mattered — not enough, anyway, to keep him from doing it. In the light of Caroline's revelation, he saw that self-questioning for what it really was — a false and vain disavowal of his *own* desire.

It was then, as he thought of the sad little cornflower hidden among the stones of the Devonshire coast, that he began to suspect he knew "who" Caroline was. Yes, he did know her, he had always known her — and he had always loved her. He stared at the door she had closed behind her, feeling gratitude deeper than he had ever known — for many things he would name later when he had more time and less fatigue. For now, just for this moment, he was simply grateful that her heart was still pure, despite all that had been done to her — done in the name of "love" for her.

* * *

At that same hour, a large number of armed horsemen rode into the city of Bath and descended on a small house there in Compton Lane.

9

The afternoon of the same day, the twenty-sixth of May

Margaret had been waiting in the hall when Caroline left the room, closing the door quietly behind her. Caroline looked so pale that Margaret was concerned.

"Caroline, are you all right?" she asked. The intuition she had had that there was some kind of bond between her niece and the priest returned. Margaret had decided that it was only imagination, or anxiety, made overly sensitive by her grief, but now she wondered.

"Yes," Caroline answered. She held her aunt's shoulders and kissed her cheek. "You will rejoice in your new priest, Aunt Margaret. He is a gift from God." Then she proceeded to her room.

Margaret looked after her for a moment, then entered the room and knelt on the pillow before Stephen. He blessed her and said, "Mrs. Anders, you don't need to confess now. Don't expect so much of yourself while you are in mourning."

But Margaret was insistent. Here was her daughter, she said, whose zeal for Christ had brought her martyrdom, yet she herself lived the lie of a coward every day.

"So you feel—what? Unworthy? Unworthy to be alive when she is not?"

"Father, my maid Eloise has more honor than I do. She deserves God's love more than I do. She is Protestant, but she is honest—not a coward."

"Ah, have you never heard of the two colors of martyrdom? Eleanor was a red martyr, killed for her faith, but there are many white martyrs now, many indeed."

"I don't understand."

"A red martyr faces death, but a white martyr must face life. Of course, death is a fearsome thing, but we know that Heaven awaits all those who die in Christ. It is a suffering that 'lasts but a little while,' as St. Paul describes it. For those who must face life instead—those like you—suffering is long. St. John faced this white martyrdom, too, you know. He lived to a very old age after all the other apostles had been martyred."

Margaret thought for a moment about red and white martyrdom. "Oh, Father, is this true?"

Stephen's heart broke for this penitent and for all those like her in England. As he said the words absolving her and made the Sign of the Cross over her bowed head, he prayed God extend that absolution to all those whose names he would never know.

She started to rise, to walk to the door, but he stopped her. "Wait, Mrs. Anders. You have not received your penance."

She stopped, embarrassed. "Oh. Yes, Father."

"Think about your maid. She has honor, an admirable but earthly virtue. You have something else. You have the Eucharist. Think about which you prefer. That's your penance."

"Thank you, Father." She turned to leave then, but when she reached the door, she turned again and said, "Father, I believe my niece is a saint."

He made no reply.

John entered then and knelt on the pillow. After the priest's blessing, he proceeded without hesitation. "My faith is weak, Father. And I am angry with God—if he exists at all." His face looked as though it were set in stone.

Stephen was surprised. "Do you mean to confess that you do not believe in God? Is that what you're telling me, John?"

"No. No, I really do—believe, I mean. But it's not like my mother's belief, or Caroline's, not like Eleanor's was—or even Thompson's."

"How is it different?"

"They would die for their faith—Eleanor did! I couldn't do that. I couldn't give up my life as my sister did. My faith, such as it is, is more like my Uncle William's, Caroline's father. We believe, yes, whatever that means, but we are both men of the world, who deal with reality. He would not die for his faith, nor would I."

Stephen closed his eyes—to hear better, as he had done with Caroline and with Margaret, to hear what John said and what he did not say. There was a long pause and silence; John became restless. Finally Stephen said, "Are you sure that you're not talking about love—and not about what you are calling your faith?"

"I don't think I understand you, Father."

"John, did our Lord die for faith? Or did he die for love?"

John stared at him. "For ... love," he said slowly.

"Think about what you've just told me before you receive Communion tomorrow. Think about your own words—not mine—not anyone else's. And ask God to help you understand what our faith really is, both your mother's *and* yours. Now, say the Act of Contrition."

After John had left, Stephen stood and removed the purple stole and folded it into the homespun. John was the last penitent until he heard Thompson later. He wanted to pray, to thank God for allowing him to hear his first confessions in England. And he knew faintly, too tired to think about it, that the confessions had not been only for the penitents, but also for himself. Of that he was certain, but he looked at the bed across the room, and he could think of nothing else. He fell across it, utterly exhausted, and sleep came too quickly for either prayer or thought.

* * *

Late that afternoon, at about the same hour that Eloise and Norma were setting out plates of cold meat on the servants' table in the Andersgate kitchen, silence had descended on the little house in Compton Lane in Bath. While lights were being kindled in the neighboring houses, it stood empty in the approaching darkness with its front door hanging askew on one hinge at the bottom of the doorway. There was just enough light in the house to see, and the neighbors who lived in the house next door, a Mr. Franklin Langtry and his wife, Nelle, made their way tentatively around the devastated parlor of Mr. Farwell's house. The shouts and clamor that had dominated the entire street were gone, as well as the armed horsemen. The house had been silent for over an hour now, and they judged it safe to go and investigate. No one was there. The house was empty.

Everything was in shambles. The seats of the parlor chairs had been ripped open, the contents of the cupboards dashed to the floor, crockery broken.

Nelle had begun to weep softly, wiping her tears with her apron skirt. "Oh, Frank, there's little enough to be grateful for, but at least young Samuel was not at home." They knew Sam to be away from home; they had heard him leave early yesterday morning on horseback. "But whatever will he do when he returns and finds this waiting for him, and his mother gone?"

"Well," replied her husband, "I can mend the door, and maybe with some help, we can get the house back in order, though it will take some time."

But Nelle had gone through the narrow passage to the little room Mr. Farwell used as a study. "Oh, la, Frank, come and see."

The room was completely destroyed. Even the inkpots had been turned over and spilled. Nothing in the room was left in one piece. Nelle was now sobbing into her apron. "Oh, Frank.

How will this ever be made right? What will they do when they come back?"

Frank looked at the chaos of the little room—even the walls had been broken open. "I don't think they'll be coming back, Nelle," he said. He put his arm around his sobbing wife's shoulders. "Come. Let's go home now."

* * *

After Thompson's confession to Stephen in the steward's house, a sealed message was delivered to him at the gate by Eloise. A woman who lived several miles north of Kefington was dying and the priest would be needed within a day or two. They decided that Stephen would leave through the tunnel for the woman's house after Mass in the morning, but he promised he would return later to be with Margaret and John a while longer.

Thompson showed him the cubbyhole of rolled maps he kept in the sacristy behind the bookcase, maps of the roads to all the Catholic homes in the area. He kept the maps in the sacristy in case there was ever any danger of a raid in his office. When Stephen returned from his visit in a few days, Thompson would show him where all the Catholic families were in Somerset—there were many—and Stephen would make plans to visit each of them. Because he would be on foot, the trip would take a long time—probably two months or more, even if he spent only a little time with each family. Some were close enough together that he could visit two in a day's time; some were more distant, and he'd need to stay overnight. The trip would take some planning. The longer stays had to be arranged so that they would occur in houses where he could be safely hidden without endangering the families who lived there.

Then they sat in his office, and Thompson talked with him about what he could expect to find at the homes he would visit—some were poor and unable to provide much for Stephen;

others were wealthy, and the families had constructed a safe place for the priest to stay, to eat and sleep. But of all the places he'd visit, Andersgate was the most comfortable and the safest, and of course, it was also where Thompson was — the place where communication began and ended.

Thompson took him into his small bedchamber next to the office, where there were two beds. "This is where you'll sleep when you're here, Father. I keep a larder over there in the corner in case you're hungry when you arrive and I'm not here at the time. But I usually know when to expect you, so if you come in from the tunnel and I'm not here, you'll find things ready for you."

Stephen was impressed. Though he knew he'd seldom be at Andersgate for any length of time, he would be almost as comfortable when he was there as he would have been at his own home. And he would be as safe as it was possible for a Catholic priest to be anywhere in England.

They had a rather long conversation then about the situation for Catholics in Somerset. Thompson had wisely followed a policy of keeping communication among Catholics to an absolute minimum, and everyone — including the Anders family — understood and accepted the ignorance that had to be imposed on them. He told Stephen that he believed whoever had informed on Father Joseph had also been the cause of the recent visitation of the queen's bishops in Kefington. Whoever it was, he said, the informer couldn't have been a Catholic. If he had been, the consequences would have been far worse for everybody. But, because the visitation yielded no real discoveries, he thought Somerset would be fairly safe for quite a long while now.

Before they left the steward's house to go to supper in the main house, Stephen decided that he would sleep that night there in Thompson's bedchamber. Not only would it be more convenient to prepare for Mass in the morning, but it would be a home for him to return to, for probably a long time in the future, and he might as well get used to being at "home."

Supper that night was as somber as dinner had been, but it was less tense. Plans had been made; everyone knew what they were to do. Mass would be said before dawn, Sam would leave with the horses directly afterward, before the servants woke. Then, after getting directions from Thompson, Stephen would leave by the tunnel to visit the dying woman some ten miles away. There was little conversation, but there was an atmosphere of peace that had not been there at dinner. Margaret was accepting Eleanor's death. She would never stop feeling the loss, just as she had never stopped missing Ben, but there were some things that mitigated her sorrow, now that she was able to think a little more clearly: Eleanor had died with little or no suffering, and most of all, she had died as a martyr for the Bride of Christ—for his Church. This latter fact did little to alleviate her grief, but she knew it was a death Eleanor would have wanted, and it gave her the courage to face the martyrdom that she herself must endure, the white martyrdom of living without her beloved daughter. And that brought her a measure of peace.

She looked down the table at Caroline and thought she must have had some sleep that afternoon. The corners of her eyes had looked pinched ever since she arrived, but now she seemed more relaxed. The gentleness that used to be so customary in her countenance had returned, but there was something else now also, something that was not customary at all—resolve. It was as though confusion had abided there before and was apparent now only by its absence. Margaret wondered what was happening to her niece, and she instinctively looked at the priest's face—but she found nothing there to answer her.

The only face lacking the peace that reigned at table was John's. Caroline had stopped him in the upstairs hallway before they came down to supper.

"John!" She held him by the arm. "I have written two letters to be posted."

"Caroline, what's the matter?" Something had happened. She seemed almost excited.

"I will tell you and Aunt Margaret about my plans after supper, for I expect to be leaving for Yorkshire on the day after tomorrow."

"Yorkshire? Why? Caroline, what on earth—?"

"I will explain everything later."

He sat now with an agitated frown as he ate his supper. What could Caroline be planning? If she was going to Yorkshire, she was going home to her father. She was leaving her husband—yet that thought was just too improbable. Unhappy as he knew she was, Caroline would be the last person he'd ever expect to make such an assertive, bold, and *disobedient* move. But at least his wonder at his cousin's action took his mind off his grief for his sister.

When supper was over, Stephen, Thompson, and Sam retired to the steward's house. Thompson made a pallet on the floor for Sam between the two beds and then went to the inner room to set up for Mass in the morning. Before Stephen could get into bed, Sam said he wanted to talk with him a bit. He was holding his cap, twisting it in his hands.

"Father, my mother wants me to be received into the Church."

"And what do you want?"

"I don't know. No—" He stopped, then sat down abruptly on the pallet at Stephen's feet. Something made it very important to be honest now, to tell the whole truth, at least this once. "That's not true. I do know. It's a lie to say that I don't know."

Stephen waited while the young man tried to gather his thoughts. Finally Sam held out the cap in his hand. "My mother made this cap for me a long time ago. It's old now, much worn, you might say. It's been through many seasons and labors, and so it's got some damage now. But it's the only one I have and the only one I want; it fits my head, keeps me warm, does what a cap should do. It is my cap. Now suppose you said to me: 'Samuel, you shall not have that cap. I do not like it.' And you took it from me and put another on my head and made me wear it, though it did not fit, was not my own, the one my mother made for me. Well, I ask you, Father, which cap is truly mine?"

Stephen laughed, "I see your meaning, Sam. Wear which cap you choose!"

"Well, that's just it now, isn't it, Father? I want my own, don't I? Just so. The Church is the Church, even if it be ragged and old. It always has been, and if Scripture is telling truth, it always will be. And so, now, you don't take it away, do you, and give us another of your own fashioning, just because you don't like the one we have, and then force us to wear it."

"So. Are you telling me that you want to be Catholic, Sam?"

"No. I mean, yes, but I cannot tell you that."

"Why not?"

"Because, Father, I am afraid," Sam answered bluntly.

"I see. You're like the Lord. He was afraid, too."

"What?"

"You know, of course, that he was human too, just like you. And scared. We can't expect to be better than he was, can we?" He smiled at Sam. "Do you think you should be holier than God himself, maybe? It's exactly there, in our fear now, in these dark days, that we share his humanity. You must not hate your fear; it must be precious to you—it's your cross."

This was a new idea for Sam. "I've got to think on that," he said. Then he stood and said he'd go and help Mr. Thompson. Stephen got undressed and went to bed. He was exhausted.

In the main house, John and Margaret sat with Caroline in her room, where she told them of her plans. She had written a letter to Edward, telling him about her faith, confessing her

deception, and asking him to divorce her. She would never return to Devonshire. Margaret and John were shocked. Divorce,
though legal in England's church, was very rare, but their shock
was not due to the thought of divorce itself; they were stunned by
Caroline, their gentle, meek, self-effacing, and beloved Caroline.

"*Why?*" asked John, who was having trouble recognizing his
cousin. She looked the same, except that she looked happier
than he had seen her in a long while. What was new was her
quiet decisiveness, her firmness.

But Margaret leapt up from her chair and embraced Caroline. "I know why," she said. "Oh, Caroline—God be praised!"

10

Caroline joined Margaret and John where they waited for her at the head of the back stairs. John supported Margaret with his arm around her waist. Without a candle, they quietly descended the narrow stairs in the darkness to the first floor of the west wing and turned into the gallery, following the route that could not be seen from any window below stairs, then onto the pathway in Margaret's rose garden. They walked the short distance to the gate hidden in the hedge at the side of Thompson's house. The gate stood open in the darkness. Locking the gate behind them, they passed through to the house and entered the narrow passage to the inner room. The faint light of flickering candles could be seen beneath the door.

Stephen was already vested for a funeral Mass, assisted by Thompson, and he was kneeling on the prie-dieu before the altar in prayer, while Sam stood to the side. Four wooden chairs were set in a line behind the prie-dieu; Thompson was kneeling beside one of them. He rose and relocked the door when they had entered the room. Each member of the Anders family genuflected before the altar and knelt for brief prayer by their chairs. Then Stephen stood and raised his hands outward, and the great gold-embroidered cross on the brocaded chasuble became visible, glowing in the light of the candles. "In nomine Patris, et Filii, et Spiritus Sancti," he sang softly as he made the Sign of the Cross.

Though Sam had never received Holy Communion, he had attended many Masses with his mother. He was always fascinated anew by the beauty of the ritual. He felt—in the plain, bare room—that he was in another place somehow, a place that was not part of the world outside. Stephen's young voice was softer and smoother than Father Tidwell's as he chanted the Scriptures, and it had a hypnotic effect on him. The low chanting, the slow movements, the dimness of the candlelight made him feel utterly still, almost like one asleep, yet he had an intense awareness of every small sound and movement.

When it was time for Holy Communion, Stephen said the prayers on behalf of himself and all those present. He bowed low and pronounced faithfully the words Christ used at the institution of the first Communion on the night before his Passion: "Hoc est enim corpus meum!" Rising then, he elevated the Host between his fingers for all to see and to adore. The very air seemed to stop; the candles ceased their flickering, and Sam held his breath.

Each communicant moved forward and knelt on the prie-dieu to receive Holy Communion. It almost seemed to Caroline that her heart had ceased to beat until she herself, the last to rise, moved forward to kneel on the deep blue velvet of the prie-dieu. She raised her face and parted her lips to receive the Host from Stephen's fingertips and closed her eyes as the Blessed Sacrament touched her tongue. The last sight she saw in that moment was the dim light of the candles in the dark room. But she knew herself to be suspended in starlight in the darkness between heaven and earth. Her lips closed. All the agony of her separateness dissolved, submerged in a sea of peace, utterly alone with her Beloved, yet one with all souls everywhere who had ever loved him, or who ever would love him, in time and eternity, in all the darkness of human history. She rose and nearly stumbled back to her chair.

Margaret looked at her niece in tenderness and wonder. She posed a wordless question to heaven, knowing as she did that she already knew the answer: *Yes.* Caroline belonged to him alone.

Sam sat in his chair to the side of the altar, frozen by a drama that he could not comprehend, unfolding before his eyes in the silence of that bare room, where every corner of space seemed filled by a holy presence. Whatever the cost, he wanted to be a part of this; there was nothing he could imagine in the world outside that could ever compare with it. He knew his answer to Father Stephen's question: *Yes.*

The peace that filled the silent room was shattered then, broken by a low, rapid whooshing sound. All eyes were wide, and all bodies became tense. The sound was that of swords cutting the hedge before the gate, then came a shot and shouts. Stephen stood frozen at the altar. He knew what Thompson would try to do, what his intention had always been if the horror ever came upon them. And he knew what he had to do to stop him.

Everyone moved at once without saying a word. Thompson was already holding the half wall of books open on its fragile hinge. He would move as many as he could into the tunnel, then take Stephen's chasuble off his shoulders and put it on himself, making sure that Stephen was in the tunnel before he closed the escape door. The dark rush of air made the candles sputter and die, and the room was in total darkness. A loud, harsh whisper came from his throat: "Father! Here! Quickly!"

But Stephen did not respond. He was moving among them, shoving them forcefully in the direction of the opening, toward the cold air of the passage in the darkness. All that was heard within the room was the swishing of skirts, the scrape of chairs on the wooden floor, and hurried footsteps. No one spoke, everyone was moving. When he thought the others were already out, Stephen's rapidly moving hands reached Thompson. He grasped Thompson's shoulders from behind and shoved him through the passage doorway before Thompson was aware of what he was doing, and the doorway closed with force as Stephen fell against the bookcase and closed the latch.

In the passageway outside the room came the thunderous sound of running boots, of voices shouting: "This way! They're in here!" And something in another language that sounded like German.

Torchlight came through the crack underneath the locked door, and he saw next to him in the darkness the glint of a dagger. "Who's there?" he asked aloud.

"I am," John's voice answered.

Then he saw the rose-colored hem of Caroline's dress. "Oh, no," he moaned, but she was already beside him, grasping his hand.

"I will not leave you," she whispered.

As the door crashed open and men and torches filled the room, the deafening crack of a pistol shot snuffed all other sound, and the dagger in John's upraised hand fell to the floor. Another shot followed that came from behind, and the man in front shouted, "Don't shoot the priest! He must be taken alive!"

There was the acrid stench of smoke as torches filled the room with light. John was lying on the floor, blood gushing through his tunic where he had been shot in the chest. Caroline lay next to him, her rose-colored silken skirt darkening slowly to deep red.

* * *

Daylight broke through the forest of Gaston Hill. Thompson and Sam, after some difficulty, had succeeded in restraining Margaret from returning to the house. Finally Thompson said he would go back to the house alone and Sam should stay there with Margaret. If it was safe for them to return, he would come back for them.

He walked quickly through a heavy early-morning fog, and when he reached the house, he found it shrouded in a deathly silence. The servants were all locked in their rooms, still hiding from the invading storm of horses, shouts, and gunfire that had wakened and terrified them during the night. In the inner room of his house, John was lying on the floor, dead, and Caroline lay next to him, wounded and moaning. The gold-embroidered chasuble lay in a crumpled heap next to the altar. Stephen was gone. The escape door had remained closed and undisturbed: The hunters had found their prey.

EPILOGUE

The fifteenth day of August 1581

Nearly three months after these events, the calmness of routine had returned to the little village of Blexton. On the Sunday following the execution of Josiah Braithlow, the little parish church of St. Anselm's was full, and attendance had remained strong ever since. As far as anyone knew, there was no more recusancy anywhere in the parish—indeed, in all of East Devonshire. By this time, most people were certain of all the facts about the case, as well as the events that had occurred during the weeks that followed: A kinswoman from Dorset came and got Mrs. Braithlow and took her away. It was said that Francis Braithlow, nineteen, had escaped to Plymouth and signed on to a ship headed for the colonies of the New World; the younger son, Philip, fifteen, had been caught and sent to a London prison. The Braithlow farm would go up for auction soon, and several farmers were already thinking of bids, though people thought that Simon Leacham would probably get it. He had become something of a local hero since he had fought against the Spanish spies in his barn on that stormy night in May.

It was believed that it was the scandal concerning his wife that had caused poor Captain Wingate to resign his commission in the navy and return to his family's seat in the Midlands. Some people, mostly the women, said they had always been suspicious that Mrs. Wingate was a secret agent of the pope anyway, and some others thought she was a Spanish spy. Someone said that as far away as the Cotswolds, a zealous preacher had held her up as an example of how the devil deceives us with beauty. But whatever her role in the sordid affair had been, Blexton concluded that "the sad business" had served to unite the people of the parish in a fervor of patriotism. It was just as Mrs. Lewis said—there's always some good in every bad thing that happens.

At the Sunday services in crowded St. Anselm's Church, Patricia Wilson listened to her husband's sermon with loving attention. People noted with admiration her expression of obvious piety and wifely pride as he preached against papist traitors, exhorting his congregation to right recognition of the sovereignty of the Queen of England and loyalty to her church. Mrs. Wilson was held in considerable esteem by the villagers, as much for her new red silk gown as for her devotion to her country and to her husband.

* * *

In Somerset, on this warm August day, Eloise was unloading her belongings from the back of a cart and carrying them into the house of her cousin in Kefington. She had been the last of the servants to leave Andersgate. Mr. Thompson had disappeared the day after Mrs. Anders's funeral—no one knew where he went.

It had been raining on the day of the funeral, a slow drizzle, and Thompson had stood next to Eloise in the rain outside the church. There was not enough room inside. It seemed to Eloise that most of the county came to the funeral of her mistress. On the last day of her life, she went walking in the forest and simply did not return. Her body had been found that evening. So many people were at the service, wearing an expression not of grief, but of loss, personal and confusing, like the discovery of a treasure only after one has lost it forever.

The people of Kefington had been shocked to learn that the Anders family were Catholics, but never again after the hanging of Kate Pettigrew would they regard Catholics as the government intended. A few years later, when the queen at last succeeded in her efforts to prod the Spanish into war, no volunteers could be found there.

* * *

On this day in the Midlands, Sir Edward Wingate slowed his tall new gelding to a walk, then allowed the horse to wander aimlessly along the lanes of the vast Wingate lands. It was a rare morning—puffs of white clouds rested calmly in a sky almost Mediterranean blue. The air was warm and still. A few remaining blackberries were overripe along the edges of the lane. A farmer stopped to allow him to pass, greeted him with "My lord," and bowed before him; Edward nodded in return. He was lord here. His holdings were very extensive, and Caroline's dowry, properly invested, would give him all the wealth and security he would ever need. He would marry again after some suitable period, and his heirs would live in peace and safety.

Caroline's letter had left him strangely unmoved at first. She confessed her religion in the letter, asking him to divorce her, and expressing the hope that he would find someone who would make him happy. She begged him to forgive her deceit. Her one request—for a divorce—he would grant with haste and ease, but the second request, forgiveness, would never be forthcoming.

His first impulse had been to burn the letter, but more clear-headed second thought informed him that he should pass it on to his solicitor. The divorce was now in progress and would clear the court very soon, having met the bishop's immediate approval—for Edward was seen as a martyr for the Church of England and a victim of Catholic treachery. He was regarded with sympathetic understanding.

This view of heroic Captain Wingate, veteran of England's struggle against Spanish villainy and victim of a Romish traitor, was a view he had chosen to share. It became history for him, because it was a history in which he himself had played no active part, had no moral responsibility. In revealing everything to him, Caroline had, as she had intended, given him knowledge of herself—but also, without intending it, she had inadvertently made Edward a mystery to himself. And he found that he preferred the view that others had of him to that mystery, which became a stone that dropped in his heart and remained there the rest of his life.

He stopped his horse on a small rise. As far as he could see in any direction, all the fields and farms, beyond the construction that had begun on his new house in the hazy distance—all of it was his. He had wealth and power that could only grow, like an empire. His prosperous future lay before him, immense and empty.

* * *

In London, at Whitehall, Lord Walsingham, private secretary to the queen, sat opposite the representatives of the Royal Treasury who surrounded the table between them. The table was strewn with many documents. Lord Walsingham was stunned at the unexpected extent of the wealth the Crown would acquire from the Anders estate in Somerset. He could hardly wait to inform Her Majesty.

* * *

And at Tyburn Tree in London, where priests were executed, Stephen tried to look for her, but he couldn't see. He thought it was the blood and sweat that blurred his vision. But there she was, in a haze, only some fifteen or twenty feet away, still and silent in the midst of the small jeering crowd—he could see her face just barely. Then he realized that his vision was not blurred, but that his sight was leaving him: he was dying. His slight body had already been racked several times. The hangman pushed the noose over his head, but he knew he would not be taken down alive for the final butchering. He would not even live long enough to be killed by the hanging.

Then, sudden as a gasp of breath, he saw her clearly. Her face was all he saw, and her tearless eyes, cornflower blue, looked into his own as directly as an arrow finds its mark. He felt his heart swell within him, with that same love that had overwhelmed him on the morning of his arrival from the sea. He knew "who" she was—she was England. Not the nation, nor the kingdom, but the soul of England, still faithful, though wounded and hidden. He had known and loved her all his life, long before he recognized her in that sad, brave, little flower surviving alone among the stones. His questions—why he had left his country, why he had returned a priest, had all been answered. He had done it for the same reason he was now dying, not for faith, but for love.

The small crowd dispersed, disappointed that the priest had died before a proper execution could take place. Caroline was among those who wandered away from Tyburn, stumbling over the cobbles back to the home of the Postens, where she and Sam were staying until tomorrow. She had already packed her few possessions and waited only for this day, this hour. Tomorrow morning, Sam would take her to Dover.

Sam would have to remain behind. Father Farwell was dead, having refused to the end to provide the militia with information on Stephen's whereabouts, but Mrs. MacDonald, Sam's mother, would be released from prison soon, ill and maimed, and he would need to be there for her. As soon as she was able to travel, the two of them would join Thompson in Yorkshire, where he was at the house of William Nelson, Caroline's father.

Thompson was establishing an underground communication network there for the priests who were arriving from the Society of Jesus. His daughter's courageous decision had worked a transformation in William Nelson. Seven years later, he would also be martyred, for having provided sanctuary for the Jesuit priests.

Tomorrow, on the sixteenth of August, Caroline would cross the gray English sea at last—for France and for the small cloistered convent in the mountains, there to remain until her own death over thirty years later. Only she among the crowd at Tyburn was not disappointed, for she had looked into Stephen's eyes as he died, and there she had seen the one she had always loved, the one to whom she had always belonged, and it was enough.

About the Author

Dena Hunt taught English at the University of New Orleans until her conversion to Christianity in 1984. Following her reception into the Roman Catholic Church, she returned to her native Georgia and taught in rural high schools for the next twenty years. It was not until after her retirement and a pilgrimage to England in 2006 that she started writing. Since then, she has published many short stories, essays, and reviews in print and online. *Treason* is her first full-length novel.

An Invitation

Reader, the book that you hold in your hands was published by Sophia Institute Press.

Sophia Institute seeks to restore man's knowledge of eternal truth, including man's knowledge of his own nature, his relation to other persons, and his relation to God.

Our press fulfills this mission by offering translations, reprints, and new publications. We offer scholarly as well as popular publications; there are works of fiction along with books that draw from all the arts and sciences of our civilization. These books afford readers a rich source of the enduring wisdom of mankind.

Sophia Institute Press is the publishing arm of the Thomas More College of Liberal Arts and Holy Spirit College. Both colleges are dedicated to providing university-level education in the Western tradition under the guiding light of Catholic teaching.

If you know a young person who might be interested in the ideas found in this book, share it. If you know a young person seeking a college that takes seriously the adventure of learning and the quest for truth, bring our institutions to his attention.

www.SophiaInstitute.com
www.ThomasMoreCollege.edu
www.HolySpiritCollege.org

SOPHIA INSTITUTE PRESS

THE PUBLISHING DIVISION OF